About Natalie Anderson

Natalie adores a happy ending, which is why she always reads the back of a book first. Just to be sure. So you can be sure you've got a happy ending in your hands right now—because she promises nothing less. Along with happy endings, she loves peppermint-filled dark chocolate, pineapple juice and extremely long showers. Not to mention spending hours teasing her imaginary friends with dating dilemmas. She tends to torment them before eventually relenting and offering—you guessed it—a happy ending. She lives in Christchurch, New Zealand, with her gorgeous husband and four fabulous children.

If, like her, you love a happy ending, be sure to come and say hi on facebook/authornataliea and on Twitter @authornataliea, or her website/blog: **www.natalie-anderson.com**

Blame it on the Bikini

Natalie Anderson

First published in Great Britain 2012
by Mills & Boon, an imprint of Harlequin (UK) Limited.
Harlequin (UK) Limited, Eton House, 18-24 Paradise Road,
Richmond, Surrey TW9 1SR

© Natalie Anderson 2012

ISBN: 978 0 263 22846 5

Harlequin (UK) policy is to use papers that are natural, renewable
and recyclable products and made from wood grown in sustainable
forests. The logging and manufacturing process conform to the
legal environmental regulations of the country of origin.

Printed and bound in Great Britain
by CPI Antony Rowe, Chippenham, Wiltshire

Also by Natalie Anderson

Waking Up in the Wrong Bed
First Time Lucky?
Nice Girls Finish Last
Dating and Other Dangers
The End of Faking It
Walk on the Wild Side
Unbuttoned by Her Maverick Boss*
Caught on Camera with the CEO*
To Love, Honour and Disobey

*Part of the **Hot Under the Collar** duet

**Did you know these are also available as eBooks?
Visit www.millsandboon.co.uk**

For Dave, Dave and Gungy:

Thank you so much for giving up time in your precious weekends to help construct 'The Plotting Shed'— without that wonderful room of my own I don't think Brad and Mya's story would ever have been finished!

I truly appreciate your kindness and generosity

(and that of Bridge and Kat for kid duty!!!)

CHAPTER ONE

Can I get away with it?

It was harder than you'd think to take a picture of yourself in a small, enclosed space wearing nothing but a bikini. Biting back the giggle, Mya Campbell peered at her latest effort. The flash had created a big white space over at least half the screen, obscuring most of her reflection, and what you could see was more dork than glam.

With a muffled snort—a combination of frustration and laughter—she deleted it and twisted in front of the mirror, trying for another. Her teeth pinched her lower lip as she glanced at the result—maybe the skinny-straps scarlet number was a step too far?

'Is everything okay?' the clearly suspicious sales assistant called through the curtain, her iced tone snootier than her brittle perfect appearance.

'Fine, thanks.' Mya fumbled, quickly taking another snap before the woman yanked back the curtain. She needed to get it away before being—ah—busted.

Both she and the assistant knew she couldn't afford any of these astronomically priced designer swimsuits. But that long-suppressed imp inside her liked a dress-up and it had been so long and if she were to have such a thing as a summer holiday, then she'd really love one of these little, very little things…

Giggles erupted as she tried to send the text. Her fingertips slipped she shook so hard. She was such an idiot. Typos abounded and she tapped faster as she heard the assistant return.

'Are you sure you don't need any help?'

She needed help all right. Professional help from those people in white coats. Too late now, the soft whooshing sound confirmed her message had gone. And she couldn't afford this scrap of spandex anyway.

'Thanks, but no, I don't think this style is really me.' Of course it wasn't. She tossed the phone into her open bag on the floor and began the contortions required to get out of the tiny bikini. She caught a glimpse of herself bent double and at that point she blushed. The bikini was basically indecent. Would she never learn that bodies like hers were not built for tiny two pieces? She'd bend to pull off her shoes at the beach and instantly fall out of a top like this. Not remotely useful for swimming. She'd have to lie still and pose, and that just wasn't her. Mind you, a summer holiday wasn't for her this year either.

And never in a million years would she send such a picture to anyone other than her best friend and all-around pain in the butt, Lauren Davenport. But Lauren would understand—and Mya didn't need her answer now. It was a 'no' already.

Brad Davenport looked at his watch and stifled the growl of frustration. He'd had back-to-back cases in court all day, followed by this meeting that had gone on over an hour too long. He watched the bitterness between the parents, watched eleven-year-old Gage Simmons seated next to him shrivel into a smaller and smaller ball as accusations were hurled from either side of the room. The boy's parents were more interested in taking pieces out of each other and blocking each other instead of thinking about what might be best for their son. And finally Brad's legendary patience snapped.

'I think we can leave this for now,' he interrupted abruptly. 'My client needs a break. We'll reschedule for later in the week.'

He glanced around the room and the other lawyers nodded. Then he glanced at the kid, who was looking at the floor with a blank-slate expression. He'd seen it many times, had worn it himself many times—withdrawing, not showing anyone how much you hurt inside.

Yeah, it wasn't only his client who needed a break. But Brad's burden was his own fault. He'd taken on too many cases. Brad Davenport definitely had a problem saying no.

Twenty minutes later he carried the bag full of files out to his car and considered the evening ahead. He needed a blowout—some all-physical pleasure to help him relax, because right now the arguments still circled in his head. Questions he needed to ask and answer lit up like blindingly bright signs; every item on his to-do list shouted at him megaphone-style. Yeah, his head hurt. He reached for his phone and took it off mute, ready to find an energetic date for the night—someone willing, wild and happy to walk away when the fun was done.

There were a couple of voice messages, more emails, a collection of texts—including one with an attachment from a number he didn't recognise. He tapped it.

Can I get away with it?

He absorbed that accompanying message by a weird kind of osmosis, because the picture itself consumed all his attention. He could see only the side of her face, only half her smile, but that didn't matter—he was a man and there were curves in the centre of the screen. Creamy, plump breasts pushed up out of the do-me-now-or-die scarlet bra she'd squeezed into. Brad swore in amazement, his skin burning all over in immediate response. The picture cut off beneath her belly button—damn it— but he really couldn't complain. Her breasts were outstanding—lush curves that made him think...think... Actually no, he'd lost all ability to *think*.

Can I get away with it?

This doll could get away with anything she wanted.

Startled, but happily so, he slid his fingers across the screen to zoom the picture, adjusting it so it was her partially exposed face he focused on now. She was smiling as if she was only just holding back the sexiest of laughs.

Brad stilled, his heart hiccupping as disbelief stole a beat. There was only one person in the world with a smile like that. Slowly he traced her lips. Her upper lip was sensual—widening, just as the bone structure of her face widened to those sharp, high cheekbones and wide-set green eyes while her lower lip was as full, but shorter; it had to be to fit with that narrow little chin. And between those slightly mismatched lips was that telltale gap between her two front teeth. It had never been fixed. Her whole body was untainted by cosmetic procedures, indeed any kind of cosmetics.

Mya Campbell. Best friend of his wayward sister, Lauren, and persona non grata at the Davenport residence.

In that minute that Brad thought about her—the longest stretch of time he'd *ever* thought about her—a few images from the past decade haphazardly flashed through his head. Glimpses of a girl who'd been around the house often enough, but who'd hidden away whenever he or his parents were home. Who could blame her? His parents had been unwelcoming and patronising. Which of course had made Lauren push the friendship all the more. And Mya had come across as less than impressed with those in authority and less than interested in abiding by any of the normal social rules. The two of them had looked like absolute terrors. And the irony was that Mya was the most academically brilliant student in the school. An uber-geek beneath the attitude and the outrageous outfits. That was why she was *at* the school; she was the scholarship kid.

He'd only ever seen her dressed up 'properly' the once. She'd still looked sullen, exuding a kind of 'cooler-than-you' arrogance, and frankly at the time he'd been otherwise distracted by a far friendlier girl. But now he saw the all-grown-up sensuality. Now he saw the humour that he'd heard often enough but never been privy to—never been interested enough to want to be privy to. Now he saw what she'd been hiding all this time. Now the heat shot to his groin in a stab so severe he flinched. And she'd sent him…?

No. He laughed aloud at the ridiculous thought. Mya Campbell had *not* just sent him a sexy summons. She didn't even know he existed—other than as her best friend's big, distant brother. Hell, he hadn't seen her in, what, at least three years? He tapped the screen to bring it back to normal—correction, completely amazing— view. No, this playful pose wasn't for him. Which meant that certified genius Mya Campbell had actually made a mistake for once in her life. What was he going to do about it? Crucially, where was Mya now?

Questions pounded his head again, but this time they caused anticipation rather than a headache. He tossed the phone onto the passenger seat of his convertible, ignoring every other message. He put his sunglasses on, stress gone, and fired the engine. Now the night beckoned with a very amusing intrigue to unravel.

Can I get away with it?

Not this time.

The music was so loud Mya could feel the vibrations through her feet—which was saying something given her shoes had two and a half inches of sole. But she was used to the volume and she had enough experience to lip-read the orders well enough now. Shifts six days a week in one of the hottest bars in town had her able to work fast and efficient. The way she always worked. No matter what she was doing, Mya Campbell was driven to be the best.

Her phone sat snug against her thigh in the side pocket of her skinny jeans, switched to mute so it didn't interrupt her shift. The duty manager, Drew, frowned on them texting or taking calls behind the bar. Fair enough. They were too busy anyway. So she had no idea whether Lauren had got the pic or what she'd thought of it. Though, given Lauren was welded to her mobile, Mya figured there'd be an answer when she got a spare second to check. She grinned as she lined twelve shiny new shot glasses on the polished bar, thinking of Lauren's face when she saw it. She'd be appalled—she'd always shrieked over Mya's more outrageous 'statement' outfits.

'Come on, gorgeous, show us your stuff!'

Mya glanced up at the bunch of guys crowded round her end of the bar. A stag party, they'd insisted she pour the trick shots for them, not her sidekick, Jonny, down the other end of the bar. She didn't get big-headed about it—truth was Jonny had taught her the tricks and she was still working towards acing him on them. It was just these guys wanted the female factor.

She'd mixed three for them already and now was onto the finale. She enjoyed it—nothing like lighting up a dozen flaming sambucas for a bunch of wild boys who were megaphone loud in their appreciation. She flicked her wrist and poured the liquid—a running stream into each glass. Then she met the eyes of the groom and flashed him a smile.

'Are you ready?' she teased lightly.

The guys nodded and cheered in unison.

She held the lighter to the first shot glass and gently blew, igniting the rest of the line of glasses down the bar. The cheers erupted. She glanced at Jonny and winked. She'd only recently mastered that one, and she knew he was standing right where one of the fire extinguishers was kept.

Grinning, she watched them knock the shots back and slam the glasses onto the bar. Some barracked for more but she already knew the best man had other ideas. Her part in their debauched night was over; they were onto their next destination—she didn't really want to know where or how much further downhill they were going to slide.

'A thank-you kiss!' one of the guys called. 'Kiss! Kiss!'

They all chanted.

Mya just held up the lighter and flicked it so the flame shot up. She waved it slowly back and forth in front of her face. 'I wouldn't want you to get hurt,' she said with a teasing tilt of her head.

They howled and hissed like water hitting a burning element. Laughing—mostly in relief now—she watched them mobilise and work their way to the door. And that was when she saw him.

Brad *High-School-Crush* Davenport.

For a second, shock slackened every muscle and she dropped the lighter. Grasping at the last moment to stop it slipping, she accidentally caught the hot end. *Damn.* She tossed it onto the shelf below the bar and rubbed the palm of her hand on the half-apron tied round her waist. The sharp sting of that small patch of skin didn't stop her from staring spellbound schoolgirl-fashion at her former *HSC*. But that was because he was staring right at her as if she were the one and only reason he'd walked into the bar.

Good grief. She tried to stop the burn spreading to her belly because it wasn't right that one look could ignite such a reaction in her.

Back in the days when she'd believed in fairy tales, she'd also believed Brad would have been her perfect prince. Now she knew so much better: a) there were no princes, b) even if there were, she had no need for a prince and c) Brad Davenport was nowhere near perfect.

Although to be fair, he certainly looked it. Now—impossible though it might be—he looked more perfect than ever. All six feet three and a half inches of him. She knew about the half because it was written in pencil on the door-jamb in the kitchen leading to the butler's sink, along with Lauren's height and those of their mum and dad—one of the displays of Happy Familydom his mother had cultivated.

Topping the modelicious height, his dark brown hair was neatly trimmed, giving him a clean-cut, good-boy look. He was anything but good. Then there were the eyes—light brown maple-syrup eyes, with that irresistible golden tinge to them. With a single look that he'd perfected at an eyebrow-raising young age, he could get any woman to beg him to pour it all over her.

And Brad obliged. The guy had had more girlfriends than Mya had worked overtime hours. And Mya had done nothing but work since she'd badgered the local shop owner into letting her do deliveries when she was nine years old.

She tried to move but some trickster had concreted her feet to the floor. She kept staring as he walked through the bar, and with every step he came closer, her temperature lifted another degree. This despite the air-conditioning unit blasting just above the bar.

He was one of those people for whom the crowds parted, as if an invisible bulldozer were clearing the space just ahead of him. It wasn't just his height, not just his conventionally handsome face with its perfect symmetry and toothpaste-advertisement teeth, but his demeanour. He had the *presence* thing down pat. No wonder he won every case he took on. People paid attention to him whether they wanted to or not. Right now Mya wasn't the only person staring. Peripheral vision told her every woman in the bar was; so were most of the men.

She needed to pull it together. She wasn't going to be yet another woman who rolled over and begged for Brad Davenport—even if he was giving her that *look*. But why was he giving *her* that look? He'd never looked at her like that before; in fact he'd never really looked at her at all.

Her heart raced the way it did before an exam when she was in mid *'OMG I've forgotten everything'* panic. Had she entered a parallel universe and somehow turned sixteen all over again?

'Hi, Brad.' She forced a normal greeting as he stepped up to the space the stag boys had left at the bar.

'Hi, Mya.' He mirrored her casual tone—only his was genuine whereas hers was breathless fakery.

It was so unfair that the guy had been blessed with such gorgeousness. In the attractiveness exam of life, Brad scored in the top point five per cent. But it—and other blessings from birth—had utterly spoilt him. Despite her knowing this, the maple-syrup glow in those eyes continued to cook her brain to mush. She ran both hands down the front of her apron, trying to get her muscles to snap out of the spellbound lethargy. But her body had gone treacly soft inside while on the outside her skin was sizzling hot. What was she waiting for? 'What can I get you?'

He smiled, the full-bore Brad Davenport charming smile. 'A beer, please.'

'Just the one?' She flicked her hair out of her eyes with a businesslike flip of her fingers. That was better— the sooner she got moving, the more control she'd regain. And she could put herself half in the fridge while she got his beer; that would be a very good thing.

'And whatever you're having. Are you due a break soon?' He stood straight up at the bar, not leaning on it as most of the other customers did. In his dark jacket and white open-neck shirt, he looked the epitome of the 'hotshot lawyer who'd worked late'.

Mya blinked rapidly. She *was* due for her break, but she wasn't sure she wanted to have it with him around. She felt as if she was missing something about this. It was almost as if he thought she'd been expecting him. 'It's pretty busy.'

'But that stag party has left so now's a good time, right? Let me get you a drink.'

'I don't dri—'

'Water, soda, juice,' he listed effortlessly. 'There are other options.' He countered her no-drinking-on-the-job argument before she'd even got it out.

Good grief. Surely he wasn't hitting on her? No way—the guy had never noticed her before.

These days Mya was used to being hit on—she worked in a bar after all. The guys there were usually drinking alcohol, so inevitably their minds turned to sex after a time. Any woman would do; it wasn't that she was anything that special. Naturally they tried it on, and naturally she knew how to put them off. She deliberately dressed in a way that wouldn't invite attention; her plain vee-neck black tee minimised her boobs and the apron tucked round her hips covered most of her thighs in her black jeans. She did wear the platforms, but the extra couple of inches helped her ability to look customers in the eye.

She still had to look up to Brad. And right now he was looking into her eyes as if there were nothing and no one else in the room to bother with. Yeah, he was good at making a woman feel as if she were everything in his world. Very good.

'I'll have some water,' she muttered. There was zero alcohol in her system but she really needed to sober up. Not to mention cool down. She swallowed, determined to employ some easy bartender-to-customer-type conversation. 'Been a while since I've seen you. What have you been up to?'

'I've been busy with work.'

Of course, he was reputedly amazing in the courtroom, but she bet his work wasn't all he'd been busy with. The guy was legendary even at school. She and Lauren had been there a full five years after him and there'd been talk of his slayer skills. Lauren had been mega popular with all the older girls because they wanted to get to him through her.

'You need to get away from the bar to have a break,' he said once she'd set his drink in front of him.

Actually she quite liked that giant block of wood between them. She'd thought herself well over that teen crush, but all it had taken was that one look from him and she was all saucy inside. But there was a compelling glint in his eyes, and somehow she didn't manage to refuse.

As he shepherded her through the crowd, she steeled herself against the light brush of his hand on her back. She was *not* feeling remotely feminine next to his tall, muscled frame. She was *not* enjoying the bulldozer effect and seeing everyone clear out of his path and him guiding her through as if she were some princess to be protected. Surely she couldn't be that pathetic?

The balcony was darker and quieter. Of course he'd know where to find the most intimate place in an overcrowded venue. She pressed her back against the cold wall. She preferred to be able to keep an eye on the punters, and it gave her unreliable muscles some support. But in a second she realised it was a bad idea because Brad now towered in front of her. Yeah, he was all she could see and there was no way of getting around him easily.

The loud rhythm of the music was nothing on the frantic beat of her pulse in her ears. But he must be used to it—women blushing and going breathless in his company. She hoped he didn't think it was anything out of the ordinary.

'Will you excuse me a sec?' she said briskly. 'I just need to check a couple of messages.'

'Sure.'

She slipped her hand into her pocket, needing to fill in a few of her fifteen minutes and catch her breath. Besides, the imp in her wanted to know Lauren's reaction to the photo she'd sent. But there were no messages at all—which was odd given Lauren's tech-addiction. She frowned at the phone.

'Did you need to make a call?' he asked quietly.

'Do you mind? It won't take a second.' And it would fill in a few more of the fifteen minutes.

'Go for it.' Brad lifted his glass and sipped.

Mya turned slightly towards the wall and made the call.

'What did you think?' she quietly asked as soon as Lauren answered.

'Think of what?'

'The pic,' Mya mumbled into the phone, turning further away so Lauren's big, bad brother couldn't hear. 'I sent it a couple of hours ago.'

'What picture?'

'*The* pic.' Mya's heart drummed faster. She glanced at Brad. Standing straight in front of her—a little too close. His eyes flicked up from her body to her face. She didn't want him listening, but now she'd looked at him, she couldn't look away. Not when she'd seen that look in his eyes. It wasn't just maple syrup now. It was alight with something else.

'I haven't received any pic. What was it of?' Lauren laughed.

'But I sent it,' Mya said in confusion. She'd heard that whooshing sound when the message had gone. 'You must have got it.'

'Nup, nada.'

Mya's blood pounded round her body. Sweltering,

she tried to think. Because if that message hadn't gone to Lauren, then to whom had it gone?

She stared up at the guy standing closer than he ought and gradually became aware of a change in him. His eyes weren't just alive with the maple-syrup effect; no, now they were lit with unholy amusement. Why—?

Impossible.

The heat of anticipation within Mya transformed to horror in less than a heartbeat. And to make it worse, Brad suddenly smiled, hell, his shoulders actually shook—was the guy *laughing at her*?

'I definitely haven't got it,' Lauren warbled on. 'But I'm glad you rang because I haven't seen you in...'

Mya zoned out from Lauren, remembering the rush in the change room, the way she'd been giggling and not concentrating, the way her fingers had slipped over the screen...

No. Please no.

Lauren's voice and the noise from the bar all but disappeared, as if she'd dived into a swimming pool and could hear only muted, warped sound. Her stunned brain slowly cranked through the facts while the rest of her remained locked in the heat of his gaze.

Her contacts list automatically defaulted to alphabetical order. She'd never deleted all the contacts already on it either—and it was an old phone of Lauren's. No doubt her brother's number had been programmed in a long, long time ago. And *B* came before *L*. So first in the phone list?

Davenport. Brad Davenport.

CHAPTER TWO

MYA ignored the fact that Lauren was still babbling in her ear and jabbed the phone, shutting it down. She shoved it back in her pocket and tossed her head to get her fringe out of her eyes. 'It seems my phone's died,' she said with exaggerated effervescence. 'Can I borrow yours?'

Brad's silent chuckle became a quick, audible burst before he summoned the control to answer. 'Really?'

She nodded vehemently, pretending she couldn't feel the rhythmic vibrating against her thigh.

'But your phone is ringing.'

Yeah, there was no pretending she couldn't hear the shrill squawks over the beat of the bar music.

'What is that?'

'It's a recording of dolphins talking to each other,' she answered brightly before hitting him with a bald-faced lie. 'But while my ringer is working, the person on the other end can't hear me.'

'Maybe you hit mute.'

'Look, can I use it?' She dropped all pretence at perky and spoke flatly. Oh, she wanted to curl into a ball and roll behind a rock. Now. This was why he was here tonight. What had he thought? Surely he hadn't thought the picture was meant for him and he'd come to her? As if she'd called him?

Mya bit back hysterical laughter. Teen Mya would have loved Brad Davenport to hunt her down for a hook-up. Adult Mya had learned to avoid sharks. And of all the people she had to mistakenly send a picture to, it had to be her best friend's brother? Her best friend's completely *gorgeous*, speed-through-a-million-sexual-partners brother?

Brad held her gaze captive with his warm, amused one. 'But my phone cost a lot of money and I don't like the way you're holding that glass of water. I don't think my phone can survive the depths.'

Was the guy a mind-reader? Of course she wanted to drown the thing—she'd drown Brad himself if she could. Or better still, herself.

How could she have made such a mistake? This ranked as the most mortifying moment of her life. Why had she gone with the scarlet bikini with the see-through sides?

'How come you have my number anyway?' he asked lazily, confirming the worst.

'This was an old phone of Lauren's.' Mya groaned. 'She passed it on to me.'

'One of the ones she lost and made Dad replace?'

Hell, that would be right. For a while there Lauren had made her father pay—literally. 'She told me he'd given her a new one and she didn't need this one any more.' She didn't like the frown in Brad's eyes.

Yeah, she was the bad influence, wasn't she? The one who came from the wrong side of the tracks to lead Lauren astray. Did he think she abused her relationship with Lauren to get things? Lauren's parents had thought that. Indeed, Lauren *had* tried to give Mya things. Mya had refused to take most of them. The little she had, she'd hidden from her own parents. She didn't want them feeling bad that they couldn't afford those kinds of gifts—indeed any. Even then Lauren had tricked her into taking this phone and she'd taken nothing since.

And now? Now there was no dignity left in this situation. 'Would you please delete it?' she asked. Yeah, begging already.

'Never.'

Incredibly, his instant laughing response melted her but she couldn't be flattered by this. She just *couldn't*. 'It wasn't meant for you.'

'More's the pity,' he said softly. 'Do you often text pictures of yourself in underwear to your friends?'

'It wasn't *underwear*,' she said indignantly.

His chin lifted and the sound of his laughter rang out, crashing and curling over her like a wave of warmth. 'It's a bra.'

But Mya couldn't float in that tempting sea. 'It's a bikini.'

He shook his head, his brown eyes teasing. 'Sorry, Mya. It's a bra.'

She was still too mortified to be teased. 'I was in a swimwear store. I wanted Lauren's opinion on it. It was a bikini.'

'There were see-though bits.' He gestured widely and half shrugged. 'There was underwire. Looked like a bra to me.'

'You'd know because you've seen so many?' She tried to bite, but felt her blush rise higher.

'Sure,' he chuckled. 'And for the record, yes, you can definitely get away with it.'

Brad watched Mya closely and couldn't bring himself to take the polite step back despite knowing the doll was embarrassed beyond belief. But no way in hell was he ever deleting that image. She was gorgeous—far more gorgeous than he'd realised. The picture had been the teaser, but seeing her like this now? All flushed and snappy, pocket-sized but bright-eyed—he was beyond intrigued.

Her hair was swept into a ponytail. Now he remembered the colour had frequently changed. She and Lauren had spent for ever in Lauren's room, giggles emanating as they did outrageous things to their hair. Though right now, instead of hot pink and purple, Mya's hair colour looked almost natural—a light brown with slightly blonde streaks round the front. Her wickedly high cheekbones created sharp planes sloping down to that narrow little chin. Those teeth and that impish smile broke the perfection, yet were perfect themselves. The all-black ensemble was unusual for her but it didn't hide her body. Despite her slender limbs and pixie face, she wasn't boyishly slim. Her jeans were painted on, and the apron around her hips didn't wholly hide her curvy butt. As for those breasts… Plumped up by the bikini/bra in the picture, they'd been so bountiful they'd spilled over the edges. Now, disguised under that plain black tee, their silhouette was minimised. But no simple cotton covering could fully hide the softness that seemed sinfully generous in proportion to her small stature.

His heart drummed a triumphant beat. Blood pulsed, priming muscles. Because he'd seen the way she'd looked at him—the flash she hadn't been able to hide when he'd first walked into the bar. There'd been that pull, that instinctive reaction. He knew the signs—the second glances, small smiles, the heightened colour. The sparkle in the eyes, the parting of the lips. Brad Davenport also knew his worth. He knew he had a body that attracted a second glance—oh, and the cynic in him knew most women would never forget his trust fund. So he was used to being wanted and he knew when a woman wanted him.

Now the tip of her tongue briefly touched that too-wide top lip and then she bit back her smile. Yeah, she still had that gap between her two front teeth.

With just a look she'd had those stag-party guys competing to catch her close and hold her. Only she'd held them off with a few words and a hint of fire. And he wasn't thinking of the lighter flame.

Brad's entire body was on fire, and for the second time that night he gave in to impulse. He took her glass from her and put it on the table next to his.

'What are you doing?' A breathless squeak.

'We're old friends,' he said softly. 'We should greet each other properly.'

'I wouldn't have said we were *friends*.' Her voice wobbled.

He smiled at the sound. He'd stirred a small response from her, but he wanted more. And he was used to winning what he wanted. Before she could say anything more, he stepped close and caught her mouth with his.

She instantly tensed, but he kept it light. When the stiff surprise ebbed from her body—pleasingly quickly—he lifted his head a fraction and stepped closer at the same time. He flicked his tongue to feel her soft lips, tracing their uneven length, and then sealing his to hers again and tasting the delight inside her mouth. And then she kissed him back and that fire exploded. Man, Mya Campbell was a hell of a lot hotter than he'd ever thought possible.

For a split second Mya wondered if she were dreaming. Then the heat blasted into her and she knew not even *her* imagination could come up with this. She held her head up without even realising—no thought of pushing him away. Because the guy did wicked things with his tongue—sweeping it between her lips. Deeper and deeper again. Caressing her mouth as if it were the most delicious pleasure. She softened, opening more. And he stepped closer, taking more, *giving* so much more.

His chest pressed into hers. She could feel how broad and strong he was. It was a damn good thing she had the wall behind her—she was sandwiched between two solid forces and it was utterly exquisite. His mouth was rapacious now. His body insistent. Like yin and yang—hard versus the soft. And yet there was tension in her body too, that fierce need for physical fulfilment unfurling inside.

She slid her hand over his abs, the heat of him blazing through the white cotton shirt. She could feel those taut muscles and shivered at the thought of them working hard above her, beneath her—every way towards pleasure.

Her rational mind spun off into the distance while her senses took centre stage, demanding all her attention. She all but oozed into him, utterly malleable, his to twist and tease. And he did—grinding against her, kissing her mouth, her jaw, her neck and back to her mouth. She threaded her fingers through his hair, opening yet more for him.

His hand slid to the curve of her hip, lower still to her butt. He spread his fingers, pulling her hips closer to the heat of his—so she could feel his response even more. A moan escaped as she felt his thick erection pressing against her belly. So hot, so soon, this was just so crazy.

But all thought vanished as his other hand slid up from her waist, cupping her breast. She momentarily tensed, anticipating the pain—she was too sensitive for touch there. But his fingers stilled, not following through on their upward sweep; a half-second later he moved again to cup her soft flesh, avoiding her nipple. Good thing, as both were overloading already just with the pressure of his chest against hers. She relaxed against him again as she realised he somehow understood. Instead he pressed deeper—his tongue laying claim to her mouth, his body almost imprinting on hers.

And despite this oh-so-thorough kiss, she wanted so much more than this.

She moved restlessly—tiny rocking motions of her hips. It was all she could manage given how hard he was pinning her to the wall. But with every small movement she drew closer and closer to the hit of ecstasy that she suddenly needed more than anything else in the world.

It wasn't a kiss; it was a siege—he'd encircled her and demanded her surrender. It hadn't taken her long to cave at all. Her fingers curled instinctively into his cotton shirt as wicked tension gripped her. Almost at breaking point—the convulsions of ecstasy were a mere breath away.

'Excuse me!'

Mya froze and she felt Brad's arms go equally rigid. She pulled back and met his eyes—he looked as startled as she felt.

'Mya, you're way over your break time.' Drew, her boss, snapped right beside her. 'What do you think you're doing?'

All but stupefied, Mya turned and stared at her boss. She literally didn't know. Couldn't think. Couldn't answer. She was still trying to process the chemical reaction that had ignited every cell while in Brad's embrace. But as she looked at the extreme irritation on Drew's face, reality rushed back. Her boss was furious. Panic slammed the door shut on the remaining good vibes—she couldn't afford to lose this job. What on earth *had* she been thinking?

'Drew, I'm so sorry,' she said in a breathless rush, stepping further away from Brad. 'I wasn't aware of the time. I didn't—'

'No kidding,' Drew interrupted rudely, her scrambled apology having no effect on his temper. 'This is—'

'My fault.' To Mya's horror, Brad coolly interrupted Drew. 'I distracted her.'

Drew turned his glower on Brad. But within a second his expression eased a fraction as he got a good look at the man now stepping up in front of him.

Mya watched the two men square off. All of a sudden Brad seemed both taller and broader as he moved to put himself partly between her and Drew. Oh, this wasn't good—she really didn't need Brad interfering; she was on the line as it was. She could handle Drew herself without any macho-male stuff.

Brad sent her a quick glance but seemed oblivious to her wordless plea to shut the heck up and back off. Instead he turned back to Drew.

Mya held her breath but then Brad smiled—that big, easy smile, with just a hint of the 'born-to-it-all' arrogance. 'My name's Brad Davenport.' He extended his hand as if it were not in the least embarrassing that he'd just been caught kissing the brains out of Drew's employee when she should have been working. 'I want to hire out your bar.'

'Drew.' Mya's manager paused a moment and then shook Brad's hand. 'This is a popular place. I'm not sure you'll need the whole bar for one small party.'

'It's not going to be a small party. I want the whole

bar,' Brad answered calmly. 'Obviously we'll pay to secure absolute privacy for the night.'

Mya watched the change come over Drew as he assessed Brad's worth. It didn't take much to know the clothes were designer, the watch gold, the self-assurance in-built...

'I'm sure we can come to some arrangement.' Drew's demeanour changed to sycophantic in a heartbeat.

'I'm sure we can.' Brad smiled his killer smile once again. 'It should be good. This place has an atmosphere I like.'

Mya watched the Davenport charm in action as he arranged a meeting time with Drew. He got everything his own way *so* easily. Utterly used to doors swinging open—and women's legs parting on sight of that smile too. And while she was totally relieved he'd just saved her neck from the block, she was also irritated with the ease with which he'd done it. The man had everything. Money, looks, brains, charm. Had he ever known what it was to have to fight for something? To really have to work for something? Mya knew what it was to work, *hard*.

'You have two minutes,' Drew said to Mya, as if he were an emperor granting a favour to a lowly serf. 'Then back behind that bar.'

'Of course.' Mya nodded as he disappeared into the crowd. Then she turned back to Brad. 'I'm afraid you're going to have to follow through on that meeting.'

'I'm looking forward to it.' Brad didn't look at all bothered. 'I think a night here could be fun.'

Mya chose to ignore the hint of entendre in his expression. 'Have you got a reason to party?'

'Who needs a reason?' Brad shrugged.

'Because life's just one big party?'

He merely chuckled and then stepped closer. 'I'm sorry we were interrupted. Things were getting interesting there.'

But that close call had firmly grounded Mya. 'Things were getting out of hand,' she corrected, opting not to look any higher than his collar. 'I'm sorry about that. You took me by surprise.'

'Wow,' Brad said after a pause. 'I'm intrigued to think what it'll be like when I give you fair warning.'

Mya shook her head and stepped away. 'You're not getting another chance.'

She felt his hand on her elbow turning her back towards him. His hand slipped down her arm to take her fingers in his.

The touch made her look up before she thought better of it. His surprisingly intense expression incinerated her but she hauled herself from the ashes of easiness. Mya liked sex, but she preferred it within the context of some kind of relationship, not the one-night-stand scene Brad was champion of. And she was steering well clear of *any* kind of entanglement for the foreseeable future. Long-term future. She had too much else to do—like work, study and occasionally eat and sleep.

Also, this man had always had everything too easy. She'd just seen him in action—twice already tonight. He wasn't having her that way again. She truly had just been caught by surprise, and her response to him was simply a reflection of his expertise and her lack of any physical release in the last while, right?

The swirling frustration and embarrassment inside her coalesced and came out as temper. 'You thought that picture was a booty call, didn't you?' She called him out with sarcasm-coated words. 'From a woman that you haven't spoken to in at least five years?'

'Have we ever spoken?' He laughed off her accusation. 'I thought you and Lauren just paraded around fake-Goth-style and giggled behind closed doors. Interesting to think what was really going on behind those doors given the pictures you send each other. Thinking about it, you two went to prom together, didn't you?'

'With her boyfriend,' Mya answered.

'Oh, a threesome.' Brad laughed harder.

'If you remember, she tried to get you to take me.'

'Oh, yeah.' His eyes widened as he thought about it. 'That's right.'

Unlike him, Mya had *never* forgotten what for her had been the most mortifying moment of that night. He'd been home from university. He'd had some silvery-blonde girlfriend with him. Tall and sleek, she'd had the obligatory blue eyes and the label clothes and the 'born to it all' attitude. Mya had hated her on sight. The girlfriend had spent most of the time spread on a sofa being kissed to glory by Brad.

'You were wearing one of Lauren's dresses,' he said slowly.

'Yes.' She was amazed he'd now remembered that detail. Mya had butchered one of Lauren's many formal dresses. A soft, pretty pink dress—never a colour she'd normally wear. She'd taken to it with a pair of scissors and completely cut away the back and secured it with long, trailing ribbons. She'd been aiming for a soft romantic look.

It was the dress that she'd hoped might garner her the attention she'd thought she'd wanted. All she'd wanted to do was fit in—to be popular and accepted. To be just like the rest of them and *not* different for once. She'd wanted it to all be easy. But it was never as easy as a change of clothes. Make-overs didn't change the person underneath. She hadn't just been sixteen and never been kissed. She'd made it all the way to eighteen and first-year uni before that honour had fallen to a fellow student who'd seemed sweet enough until he'd had what he wanted.

But back at that night of the dance, she'd had the whole prom fantasy. What wallflower schoolgirl didn't? The one where the hottest guy in school asked her to dance and it was all perfect and ended with a kiss. Or the super-hot brother of the best friend asked her? Yeah, she'd been such a cliché. And she'd felt like a princess for all of five minutes, until Brad had ignored her. She'd been pretty and dressed up and hadn't even been able to turn the head of the most sexually hungry male she knew back then.

'You were too busy wearing that blonde to answer at the time,' Mya said dryly.

The dimple in his cheek deepened. 'Yeah, that's right.'

He hadn't appreciated his younger sister's interruption. Mya had seen the raw lust in him, the tease, the firmness with which he pulled the girl onto his lap—his strong arm wrapped around her waist, his confident hand close to her breast. And for a few minutes, she'd wanted to be that girl. Now for five minutes she had been. And it was better than any fantasy.

Mya sucked up her stupidity and turned her self-scorn towards him instead. 'That's all irrelevant anyway. What's really the issue here is how pathetically horn dog you are. You get a look at a woman in her *bikini* and you're suddenly hot for her? When you've never so much as looked at her in the last decade?'

Amusement still burned in his eyes. 'You were a child a decade ago.'

'It's still pathetic.' And frankly, insulting.

'Maybe that prom night isn't so irrelevant at all.' His smile widened. 'Did you have a crush on me back in high school? Your best friend's older brother?'

She gaped.

'Because,' he leaned closer and drawled outrageously, 'you wouldn't have been the only one.'

Hell, the guy had an ego. Unfortunately what he'd said was true. There were several girls who'd done the faux-friendship thing to Lauren just to get close to her brother. Mya shook her head and denied him anyway. 'Girls that age are at the mercy of hormones just as boys are and they fixate on the nearest object. Their fixating on you was probably more a matter of locality than your attractiveness.'

He grinned wolfishly. 'So if it wasn't me your hormones fixed on, then who?'

'I didn't have the time.'

'Everybody has the time.' He moved closer as his voice dropped to an intimate whisper. 'Who did you used to dream of?'

'No one.'

'So rebellious on the outside, such a square inside.' He shook his head.

Mya gritted her teeth.

'No wonder you erupted with one touch—you've been repressed too long.'

Mya couldn't answer because that was actually true. She'd been without too long; that was the reason she'd inhaled his touch like an attention-starved animal.

'Did you wish I'd said yes to Lauren and taken you to the ball? Is that why you're trying to cut me down now? Did I burst your love-struck teen bubble?'

He was so close to the mark it was mortifying. But she'd never, ever admit it. 'I'm sure you've burst many

poor girls' bubbles, but you never burst mine.' Mya
willed a languid tone. 'Fact is I've always seen through
your charm to what you really are.'

'And what am I?'

'Selfish, spoilt, arrogant. Insufferable.'

'Is that all?' He paused a moment. 'You don't want
to add some more about how unattractive you find me?'

Very funny. 'You're so up yourself it's unbelievable.'

'But you still want me.' He breathed out and then
laughed. 'You're never going to be able to deny it. Not
when you kissed me like that.'

'You were the one who kissed me.' Cross, she licked
her extremely dry lips.

'It started that way but within two seconds you were
clawing my shirt off.'

'I was trying to push you away.'

The rogue laughed harder. Mya pulled her hand free
of his grip and strode back through to the bar. She got
behind it and found he was right there in front of her,
waiting to be served—and still annoyingly amused.

'You have to go now,' she told him firmly, determined
not to let that smile affect her. 'I have work to do.' She
pulled out a chopping board, some lemons and a knife
to prove it.

'No.' He shook his head. 'I need you more than ever
now.'

Yeah, right. He'd never needed her before. And while
she didn't want to think he'd kissed her on a whim, the
fact was he had. He'd never wanted to kiss her before,
remember? The guy who had his pick of every woman
in every room in the world hadn't noticed her until she
was hardly dressed. It really didn't do much for her ego.
And even less for his character. It showed he was sim-

ply attracted to the lowest common denominator—bared flesh.

He shook his head in mock despair. 'You suspect my motivation.'

'Your reputation does precede you.' She maintained her cool. 'And all you've said and done so far tonight merely confirms the worst.'

'Actually, Mya, I really do need you.' His expression went serious. 'I'm not just going to hire out the bar. I'm going to hire you.'

CHAPTER THREE

'I'M NOT interested.' Mya was telling herself that over and over but her body wasn't listening. Her pulse still pounded, her ears still attuned to every nuance in his words. But her ego was piqued. He'd kissed her only after seeing her breasts in a skimpy bikini—and now he wanted to *hire* her? For what exactly?

'Sure you are.' He winked. 'I have to have a party now and you're the perfect person to organise it for poor helpless me.'

She shook her head. 'Poor and helpless are the antithesis of what you are. You don't need anyone, let alone me.'

He grinned, obviously appreciating the unvarnished truth, but behind the smiling eyes she sensed his brain was whizzing. Yeah, the guy was wickedly calculating. And far too together already after the kiss that had shattered her. She needed to keep her guard well up.

'Lauren's finished her degree,' he said.

Momentarily thrown by the change in topic, Mya blinked. Then she nodded, but said nothing. If she hadn't been such an idiot, she'd have been a lot nearer to finishing her degree too.

'For a while there it didn't seem likely she'd even finish high school let alone a university degree,' he added.

He was right. When Mya had started at that school,

Lauren's wild streak had been on the verge of going septic and that hadn't been in the perfect Davenport family plan at all. They were all graduates with successful careers—and expected Lauren to achieve the same. Whereas Mya was the *only* one in her family to have finished school. She was supposed to be the first in the family to finish a degree too. Honours no less, having won a prestigious scholarship. Except she'd screwed it up, and now she doubted that she'd ever deserved it. But she'd finish her degree all on her own account—independence was now everything to her. This time she was taking the lead from Lauren. So she nodded. 'She defied everyone's expectations and did it. Brilliantly too.'

There was a pause and she couldn't help glancing at him. And then they both laughed at that one unbelievable aspect of Lauren's success.

'It's more than a little ironic, don't you think?' he said, his face lightening completely. 'That she almost dropped out and now she's going to be a teacher?'

'She'll be a dragon too, I bet.' Mya bit her lip but couldn't quite hold back the chuckle. 'Super-strict. She won't put up with any illegal nail polish.' Back in the day, Mya and Lauren had broken more than the nail-polish rules. Their favourite look had been purple splatter.

'So we'll have the party for her. It's as good an excuse as any,' Brad said confidently. 'Exam results are out. It's not long until Christmas. Many of her friends are going overseas and won't be back for her graduation ceremony next year. She's worked hard for a long while.' He faced her square on again. 'So we'll surprise her.'

'You're going to have it as a surprise?' Mya asked. 'You want me to distract her?' She'd be happy to sneak Lauren out and be there for the big surprise moment.

But he was shaking his head. 'I want you to organise it.'

Mya's enthusiasm burst like a kid's balloon encountering the prick of a needle. Of course he did. He had to have this party but she'd be the one copping all the extra work to get it ready? Her ego suffered another blow—and more importantly she just didn't have the time to do it. 'Isn't partying *your* area of expertise?'

'Darling, I've never *planned* a party. I *am* the party.' He mimicked her emphasis.

'Oh, please.'

'Who better to arrange it than my sister's best friend? I said I'll hire you. You'll be paid.'

She bridled. 'I'm not taking money from you. I'm her *friend*.' The thought of him paying for her services irked her. She'd always put in an honest day's work but the thought of *Brad* owning her time spiked her hackles.

'I'll get in a planner instead.' He shrugged.

Now she was even more ticked. He was too used to getting everything his own way. 'You think you can just throw some money on the table and have some flash event happen? Lauren wouldn't want some impersonal, chic party put together by cutesy PR girls she doesn't even know.' Mya shook her head. 'Wouldn't it mean more to her if *you* put in some personal effort? She doesn't like cookie-cutter perfection.' Lauren had had so many things bought for her—by impersonal secretaries. She liked the individual—that was part of what had drawn her and Mya so close.

He looked sceptical. 'You think I should choose the colour scheme and the canapés?'

'Why not?' she asked blandly.

'You're not tempted by an unlimited budget and licence to do anything? Most women would love that, right?'

'I'm not like most women. Nor is Lauren. You should organise it—it's your idea.' She sent him a cutting glance. 'Or are you too selfish to spend time on her?'

He laughed. 'Sweetheart, every human on this planet is selfish,' he said. 'We all do what's ultimately best for ourselves. I am doing this for very selfish reasons and not many of them to do with Lauren herself. It's mainly so *I* don't have to deal with my mother's hand-wringing and a frozen dinner out with my parents to celebrate Lauren's graduation. And so *you* don't get in trouble with your boss and take it out on me. Does that make me a bad person?'

Heat ricocheted round her body like a jet of boiling oil as she saw the intense look in his eye. He didn't want her to think badly of him? And he *was* doing this to prevent her from getting in trouble. 'No,' she conceded.

'You have to help me,' he said softly.

That was one step too far. 'We wouldn't be in this position if you hadn't kissed me.' She tried to argue back but felt herself slipping. 'You created this problem. You don't need me.'

'Do I have the names and numbers of half her friends? No. I don't know all her university mates the way you do. Of course I need your help.'

Silent, she looked at him.

'*I'm* thinking of Lauren. Are *you*?' he jeered.

She sighed. 'For Lauren's sake, I'll help. But you're not paying me.'

'What a good friend you are,' he teased.

'I am, actually,' she declared.

'We all do what is best for *ourselves*,' he murmured with a shake of his head. 'Wasn't insisting I be actively involved in the planning really because *you* wanted to spend more time with *me*?'

She gaped—how did he turn that one around? 'No. I'm only thinking of Lauren.' She vehemently denied that tendril of excitement curling through her innards at the thought of spending time with him. He had an outsize ego that needed stripping. 'You think you're irresistible, don't you?'

'Experience has led me to believe that's often the case.'

His eyes were glinting. He might be laughing, but she suspected part of him meant it. *Outrageous* wasn't the word. The guy needed taking down a peg or forty. 'Not in *this* case.'

'No?' He chuckled, radiating good humour. 'So that blush is pure annoyance? Then you've nothing to worry about, right? We can organise Lauren's party together because you can resist me no problem.'

Could she resist him? For a second Mya wondered and then her fighting spirit came to the fore. Of *course* she could. 'No problem at all.'

He leaned closer. 'I'm sorry I haven't seen much of you in recent years.'

'Maybe you should have turned up to a couple of Lauren's birthday parties.'

He winced, hand to his chest. 'I was overseas.'

She knew he'd studied further overseas before coming back and setting up his own practice. 'So convenient. For work, was it? You learned well from your father.'

'Meaning?'

'Doesn't *he* use work for emotional avoidance too? Earns millions to buy the things to make up for it.' Lauren had been given so many *things* and none of them what she'd truly yearned for.

The laughing glint vanished from Brad's eyes. 'Formed a few judgments over the years, haven't you?'

Mya realised she might have gone more than a little far. 'I'm sorry, that was out of line. I'll always be grateful for the kindness your parents showed me,' she said stiltedly, embarrassed at her rudeness.

But he laughed again, the devil dancing back in his eyes. 'Their *kindness*?'

Okay, maybe he did remember the ultra-frosty welcome she'd got for the first year or three that she and Lauren hung out. 'They didn't ban me from their home.' Even though she knew they'd wanted to. Now they realised they owed Mya something.

'Don't worry about it. I know even better than you what a mess it was.'

He'd certainly left home the second he could. Mya had been the one who'd spent every afternoon after school with Lauren in that house. She and Lauren hid up in Lauren's suite, laughing and ignoring the frozen misery downstairs. The false image of the perfect family. 'But Lauren's the one who's made the conscious effort to be different from how she was raised.'

'You're saying I've not?'

Mya shrugged. 'You're the mini-me lawyer.'

'You do know my father and I practise vastly different types of law. I'm not in his firm.'

Blandly she picked up a glass and polished it. That didn't mean anything.

'What, all lawyers are the same?' He snorted. 'I don't do anything he does. I work with kids.'

She knew this, and at this precise moment she point-blank refused to be impressed by it. 'You think your save-the-children heroic-lawyer act somehow ameliorates your womanising ways?' Because Brad *was* a womaniser. Just like his father.

'Doesn't it?'

See, he didn't even deny the charge. 'You think? Yeah, that's probably why you do child advocacy,' she mused. 'To score the chicks by showing your sensitive side.'

He laughed, a loud burst of genuine humour that had her smiling back in automatic response.

'That's an interesting take. I've never really thought about it that way.' He shrugged. 'But even if it does give me some chick-points, at least I've done something with my life that's useful. Is igniting alcohol for party boys useful?'

She shifted uncomfortably. Serving drinks was a means to an end. But she managed a smooth reply. 'Helping people relax is a skill.'

His brows shot up. 'I'm not sure you're that good at helping guys *relax*.'

She met his gaze and felt the intensity pull between them again.

'Are you still at university or are you finished now?' He broke the silence, looking down and toying with the pile of postcards on the edge of the bar.

'I'm there part-time this year.'

'Studying what?'

'A double degree. Law and commerce.'

'Law and commerce?' he repeated. 'So you're going to become a greedy capitalist like my evil father and me?' He laughed. She didn't blame him, given her stabbing disapproval mere seconds ago. 'You're enjoying it?'

'Of course,' she said stiffly.

'And the plan?'

'A job in one of the top-five firms, of course.'

'Speciality?'

'Corporate.'

'You mean like banking? Counting beans? Helping companies raid others and earning yourself wads of cash in the process?'

'Nothing wrong with wanting to earn a decent wage in a job where you can sit down.' She walked away to serve the customers she'd been ignoring too long. Her need to achieve wasn't something trust-fund-son over there could understand. She needed money—not for a giant flat-screen TV and a house with a lap-pool and overseas jaunts. She needed a new house, yes, but not for herself. For her parents.

She was conscious of his gaze still on her as he sat now nursing something non-alcoholic and taking in the scene. As she glanced over, she saw his eyes held a hint of bleak strain. Was it possible that behind the playboy façade, the guy was actually *tired*?

But he didn't leave. Even when the bar got quieter and they'd turned the music down a notch. In another ten minutes the lights would brighten to encourage the stragglers out of the dark corners. Mya felt him watching her, felt her fingers go butter-slippery. She kept thinking about the kiss; heat came in waves—when memory swept over control. She couldn't stay away when he signalled her over to his end of the bar.

'I've been thinking about the drinks for Lauren's party,' he said easily. 'It would be good to offer something different, right? Not just the usual.'

So that was why he was still sitting there? He was party planning? Not surreptitiously watching her at all?

'There you go, see?' Mya said brightly, masking how deflated she suddenly felt. 'You'll organise a brilliant party. You don't need me.'

'I need your expertise,' he countered blandly. 'I don't think I can ignite alcohol.'

No, but he could ignite other things with a mere look. Mya pulled her head together and focused on the task at hand. 'You want me to come up with a couple of Lauren-inspired cocktails?'

'They're the house speciality, right? So, yeah, make up some new ones, give them a cute name, we'll put them up on the blackboard.' He chuckled. 'Something that'll be good fun to watch the bartender make. Definitely use a bit of fire.'

'And ice,' she answered, then turned away to scoop crushed ice into a glass and wished she could put herself in with it. How could she be this hot? Maybe it was a bug?

'What would you use to make her cocktail?' he asked idly. 'What kind of spirit is Lauren?'

She took the question seriously. 'Classic bones, quirky overtones. A combination that you wouldn't expect.'

She turned her back to him and looked at the rows and rows of gleaming bottles. Reached up and grabbed a few and put them on the bar beside Brad. Then she poured. 'Her cocktail would need to be layered.' Carefully she bent and made sure each layer sat properly on the next. 'Unexpected but delicious.' She smiled to herself as she added a few drops of another few things. Then she straightened and looked at him expectantly.

He just held her gaze.

Finally she broke the silence. 'You don't want to try it?'

He studied the vivid blue, orange and green liquid in the glass in front of him. 'Not unless you try it first. It looks like poison to me. Too many ingredients.'

'I don't drink on the job.' She smiled sweetly. 'Are you too scared?'

'Don't think you can goad me into doing what you want,' he said softly. But he picked up the glass and took a small sip. He inhaled deeply after swallowing the liquid fire. 'That's surprisingly good.'

'Yes,' Mya said smugly. 'Just like Lauren.'

He grinned his appreciation. 'All right, clever clogs, what cocktail would you put together for me?'

Oh, that was easy. She picked up a bottle and put it on the bar.

He stared at it, aghast. 'You're calling me a boring old malt?'

'It needs nothing else. Overpowering enough on its own.'

'Well, you're wrong. There's another like that that's more me than a single malt.'

'What's that?'

'Tequila. Lethal, best with a little salt and a twist of something tart like one of your lemons.'

She rolled her eyes.

'And what are you?' He laughed. 'Brandy? Vodka? Maudlin gin?'

'None. I don't have time.'

'You should make time. You shouldn't work so hard.'

'Needs must.' She shrugged it off lightly. 'And you have to leave now so I can close up the bar.'

'Have lunch with me tomorrow. We can brainstorm ideas.'

She should have said yes to organising the party on her own. Why had she thought he ought to have active involvement? 'I'm at class tomorrow. I'm doing summer school.' She'd be in summer school for the next three years.

'Okay, breakfast, then.'

She shook her head. 'I'm working.'

'This place is open all night?' His brows lifted.

'I work in a café in the mornings and some other shifts that fit around my classes and the bar work.'

'And you work here every night?'

'Not on Sundays.'

'Where do you work on a Sunday—the café?'

She nodded, looking up in time to see his quick frown. She rolled her eyes. Yes, she worked hard; that was what people did when they had to. Eating was essential after all.

'Why didn't you take a summer internship?'

She turned and put all the bottles back in their places on the shelves. The summer internships at prestigious law firms in the city were sought after. Often they led to permanent job offers once degrees were completed. But she wasn't going there again, not until her final year of study and she'd recovered her grade average. Not to mention her dignity. 'I need to keep going with my studies and, believe it or not, I earn more in the bar.'

'You get good tips?'

'Really good.' She rinsed her hands again and wiped down the bench.

'You might get more if you let some more of that red lace stuff show.' He glanced down the bar. 'One thing we are going to do for the party is have better bartender outfits. You'd never guess what you wear beneath the undertaker's uniform you've got going on in here.'

Heat scorched her cheeks again. Once again, why had she picked that wretched scarlet bikini? He was never going to let her forget it. 'This is what we all wear in the bar. It's simple, efficient and looks smart.'

'It's deadly dull and doesn't make the most of your assets. Not like that red underneath it.'

'It's not underneath it.'

'You took it off?' He looked appalled. 'Why on earth did you take it off?'

'It was a *bikini*,' she said, goaded. She closed her eyes and breathed deep to stop herself laughing. His wicked smile suggested he knew she was close to it anyway. She looked at him. Not at all sorry he had to shell out however many tens of thousands to hire the most popular bar in town outright for a night during the busiest time of the year.

'Why do men get so fixated on lacy underwear?' she asked aloud. 'Don't you know sexy underwear is no indicator of how far a woman is prepared to go?'

'You're saying you'll go further than what your boring day-bra might indicate?' he said mildly.

'No!' she snapped.

'So you do wear boring day-bras?'

Oh, the guy was incorrigible. But, heaven help her, she couldn't help but laugh. So she'd see him some saucy talk, and raise him some flirt. She nodded with a secret smile. 'No lace.'

'Why's that?' The corner of his beautiful mouth lifted.

'No boyfriend to buy me some,' she flipped tartly and stalked away, letting the clip of her high heels underline her reply.

'You wouldn't let some guy buy you frills,' he called after her. 'You're too independent for that.'

Very true. Interesting he understood that. But she swung back to face him because she didn't want him thinking he knew it all. 'Actually it's just that they're uncomfortable.'

'They are?' His gaze lowered again.

'No woman can wear those things for more than five minutes.'

'No woman in my presence would need to.'

She ignored the comeback and cooed instead. 'I'm very sensitive. Lace hurts.' She watched his expression with amazement. Was he actually blushing? She smirked, pleased she'd finally managed to push him off his self-assured pedestal.

'How sensitive?' He walked down the side of the bar so he was close to her again. 'Can they cope with touch?'

That was when she realised his flush wasn't from embarrassment but arousal. Her body clenched, drenched in fire. 'No.'

'No?' he asked, surprised. The flush on his skin deepened.

She was burning up with a blush to match.

'Hmm. That sensitive, huh?' He looked thoughtful. 'What other bits are too sensitive?'

She couldn't look away from the teasing intimacy in his eyes. The intense drive of his words melted her. She hadn't meant this to get so personal. She'd been out to tease him. Only her too-sensitive bits were shrieking right now, liquefying in the heat he was conjuring—his words locking her in a lit crucible.

'Must make it difficult for you,' he said softly. 'I bet you pull away. You can't just go with it.' He looked at her speculatively. 'Just the way you pulled back from me before.'

She was so hot, her soul singed by words alone. She couldn't even answer. Because in truth? He was right.

'Seems to me you need some practice coping.'

She shook her head. 'I'm not inexperienced.' And

she definitely didn't need to get any more experience by playing with him.

His mouth curved in disbelief. 'Aren't you?'

Well, okay, she wasn't as experienced as *him*. She lifted her head proudly. 'I've had boyfriends.' Jerks, the pair of them.

'Yeah, but you've never been with me.'

'And you're that amazing?' she asked, managing a tone of utter skepticism, which was quite something given her wayward hormones were shrieking that *yes, he was that amazing!*

His expression was pure intent. 'You'll have to wait and see.'

'You're so obnoxious.' She recovered her sass, more determined than ever to shoot him down. 'Why would I want to have sex with a guy who's been with every other girl in the city?'

'Not *every* other girl,' he protested. 'But I don't see anything wrong with sharing the love,' he added. 'If you have too much sex with one woman, she starts to get funny ideas. Better to have sex with too many women. Safer.'

'Oh, real safe.' She rolled her eyes. But he wasn't denying it. Brad Davenport wasn't a commitment kind of guy. He was a playboy.

He reached across the bar and ran a finger down her arm. Electricity sparked every millimetre of the way. She saw it. He saw it. There was no denying it. So she didn't.

'This isn't anything more than lust.' She turned and literally burrowed out more ice from the freezer.

'So what?' he calmly said behind her. 'It's still worth exploring.'

'Even if I agree there's chemistry, I'm not sure I can

bear to feed your over-bloated ego by saying yes.' But the feeling the guy could inspire with just a look?

'You'll always regret it if you don't,' he insisted.

'And probably regret it if I do.'

'Damned either way, then,' he said with a laugh. 'You might as well have the good moment and enjoy it.'

'Moment?' She suppressed the squeeze her muscles had in response to his laugh. 'As in singular? What are you going for here, some orgasmic snuffle?'

'You don't need to worry. I'll take care of you.'

'I don't need anybody to take care of me,' she denied, affronted.

'Really?'

Narrow-eyed, she watched him draw closer. It seemed to her there might be an imbalance of attraction here. Was it all about her wanting him? Or was the chemistry as insane for him as it was for her?

'Maybe you don't. But you keep thinking about that kiss,' he said. 'I can tell.'

She was shaking her head already but when she went to deny it he put his finger back on her mouth.

'You can't hide it. I see it in your eyes. It's the same for me,' he said simply. 'I want to kiss you again.'

'Brad—'

He straightened. 'I accept that you're saying no, for now, but don't deny that the desire is there.'

'I haven't kissed anyone in a while.' She shrugged. 'What happened before was merely a reaction to that.'

He shook his head. 'You were every bit as into it as I was. You're as "all or nothing" in your approach to life. It's just that you go for nothing and I go for all.'

'Have you ever managed nothing?'

'I am right now.'

'Really.' Not a question, more an expression of disbelief. 'Almost two hours with nothing?'

'Nothing,' he said, as if it wasn't an experience he was enjoying. 'Not so much as an eyelash flutter since you.'

Mya chuckled and this time she reached across, clasping his wrist as if she feared he was about to have a heart attack. 'How are *you* coping?'

'Moment by moment.' He clapped his hand over hers. 'But I'm quietly confident.'

'Quietly?' she mocked. She leaned across the bar again and gave him some advice. 'You shouldn't hype yourself up so much. It'll end up a disappointment.'

'What orgasm was ever a disappointment?'

She tried so hard not to blush. 'Is that all it is for you? The momentary thrill?'

'It's pretty much up there, yeah,' he drawled. 'I won't lie.' He lifted her hand with his and pressed her palm to his heart. 'I fancy you.' He paused. 'Now, can you speak with the same kind of honesty?'

For a moment she couldn't answer as she absorbed the strong, regular thud of his heartbeat. But while the moments of orgasm might feel good, it was the moments afterwards she was more worried about. She curled her fingers into a fist and pulled away from him. 'I'm not on trial here.'

'You're a coward,' he accused. 'Is having fun so wrong?'

Mya answered with absolute honesty. 'Not wrong. Inconvenient.'

'Never inconvenient. You need to sort your priorities.'

She shook her head and laughed. 'Oh, no, I have my priorities *exactly* right.'

No burst of heat was going to blow her balloon off course.

CHAPTER FOUR

THE next night Brad watched Mya stride into the all but empty bar like a bounty hunter on a hot trail. A satchel hung over her shoulder, she'd poured herself back into the black jeans, and her fiercely swept up hair all spelt *business* to him. The bar wasn't officially open yet, but she was here to work, and anyone watching would know it.

No Messing Around Mya.

He bit back the amusement, because he was going to mess with Mya. He knew he had to play it carefully or she'd block him the way she'd blocked all those other guys at the bar. But he knew the party was a brilliant idea, and having to work with her to plan it? Genius. Because he hadn't felt heat in nothing but a kiss in for ever. The chemistry between them had kept him awake and rock hard all hours. He'd never felt the thrill of the chase like this. Then again, he hadn't *had* to chase like this. He watched closely to see her reaction when she saw him but her face remained an expressionless mask—too expressionless. Now, that took effort.

Good. If she had to work hard to hide her reaction to him, that meant her reaction was extreme. As was his to her. But he wasn't going to hide it. No, he was all about having fun and being up front.

'Hi, darling,' he called, hoping to raise a spark.

She didn't answer until she'd reached the bar and then it was with a mocking coo. 'Have you forgotten my name? I'm Mya.'

'I can't call you "darling"?' He propped an elbow on the broad expanse of highly polished wood.

'I'm suspicious of men who rely on pet names.' She moved to put the bar between them. 'I wonder if it's because they can't remember the name of the woman they're with.'

He smiled, enjoying the way she was so determined to put him in his place.

'You've been guilty of it, haven't you?' She raised her brows and said it as a statement of fact, not a question.

He always remembered a woman's name at the time, but a few months later? Yeah, he'd better plead the fifth. With growing disappointment he watched her wind the apron round her waist, hiding how well her thighs were shown off in the spray-on jeans.

'We're not open yet.' She turned to face him. 'So I can't serve you.'

'It's all right.' Brad nodded at his half-empty glass. 'Your boss already has. I've been talking with him about the party. Saturday after next. That okay for you?'

Her teeth worried her lower lip as a frown creased her forehead. 'I'll need to talk to Drew. I'm rostered to work that night.'

'Not any more. It's already sorted. You're there as a guest, not a bartender.'

That little frown didn't lighten. 'Yes, but—'

'You work every night,' he interrupted. 'You're not going to take a night off for your best friend's surprise party?'

'Of course I am.'

'Then there's no problem, is there?'

'No, but you didn't need to arrange that for me.' Her vibrant green eyes rested on him, still frustratingly cool.

Was that what bothered her? Him interfering? Fair enough. 'I thought it would help,' he explained honestly. 'I wanted your boss to understand that he couldn't call on you at all that night and that I was willing to pay for extra staff.'

'And that's wonderful of you,' she said through a smile that couldn't be more fake. 'But I can handle my own requests for a night off.' She suddenly looked concerned more than cross. 'But it's very soon and very close to Christmas. You'll have to work quick to make sure people are free that night.'

'They'll be free.' Where the food and drink were free, people turned up.

'You'll need to get invitations out.' She pulled a rack of glasses from a dish-drawer beneath the counter and began stacking them onto another shelf.

He grinned, happy that she was being overly efficient. He hoped it meant he was under her skin. 'Can't I just send a text?'

'You want the whole world and his dog to turn up and drink the place dry?' She turned and gave him a pointed look. 'You'll need to have a list of bona fide invitees on the door at the very least. But you should do proper invitations.'

'Right, okay.' He nodded as if her every word were law. 'And personalised, right?'

'Right.'

Actually she was right. Lauren wasn't a store-bought-stationery kind of woman. Mya wasn't either. Brad had spent all last night wondering just what kind of woman Mya was.

'Maybe you should do the actual invitations?' he suggested. 'You're good at taking photos and stuff. You have a real eye for composition.'

She sent him a withering look before turning back to stack the glasses. 'I don't have time. I can come up with the guest list and get you some contact details, but you're going to have to put it all together.'

'Okay, I can do that.' He sighed. 'What are you thinking of? Gilt-edged cardboard things?' Never in a million years.

She flattened him with another killer cool stare. 'I think Lauren would prefer something a little more original than that.'

'I'll get to thinking, then,' he answered mock meekly.

She eyed him suspiciously this time before her gaze lifted to something behind him and brightened. 'Nice of you to turn up, Jonny,' she called. 'Everything's ready.'

'I knew I could count on you.' The tall guy who'd just walked in winked at her. 'But you need the music.' He stepped behind the bar and the relentless, rhythmic thud began.

Brad watched Mya instinctively move in time to the beat. With her natural rhythm and grace and fiendish determination, not to mention her sharp tongue and challenging eyes? He was dying here. And he wasn't getting anywhere very far, very fast.

The bar opened and the stream began. Offices weren't shutting for at least an hour yet but these people were ready to party. He didn't want to leave. Instead he watched half the other punters eye her up just as he was doing.

She and the Jonny guy made a good combo. Jonny, tattoos on display beneath the sleeves of the regulation black tee, was tanned and tall where she was pale and petite. Brad watched them banter their way through the cocktail preps. Her competitive streak was right to the fore. It amused him seeing the clinical way she observed the guy. He saw her flicking her wrist in practice, mimicking the movement of the master.

'You're almost as good as he is,' he said when she came to his end of the bar in a quiet moment.

She didn't pout at the honest assessment. Mya wouldn't want false flattery. She was too straight-up for that. 'Give me another week or two and I'll be better.'

Brad smiled. She wanted to be the best?

'The protégée wants to whip the master, but I'm not going to let that happen.' Jonny slung his arm along Mya's shoulders.

Brad immediately felt an animal response, his skin prickling at the sight of another man touching Mya—since when did he have hackles?

'Oh, it's going to happen and you know it.' Mya flicked Jonny's arm off as easily as she'd flicked off the flirty guys from the stag do the night before. 'You're running scared.'

Both Brad and Jonny chuckled and watched her swagger to a waiting customer.

'You've been teaching her?' Brad asked Jonny.

Jonny nodded. 'She's a quick learner. Focused, driven, plus she's been practising. That's how she got the job here in the first place.'

'And she wants to work here because?'

'It's the most popular bar in town.' Jonny looked at him directly. 'We get good clientele with a lot of money to spend. So we make good money. With her looks and the skill to match, she's popular.'

'Why do you help her out? You're not threatened by her?' Brad texted some mates, determined not to turn into some sad stalker type who just sat there and stared at his fixation. He certainly didn't want to feel this needle as he watched the byplay of the two bartenders. It couldn't be jealousy, could it? Never.

Jonny laughed. 'Wouldn't you rather work with her than some guy?' he pointed out with a sly smile. 'We work well together—people like the competition. Some like to look at her, others like to look at me.' He turned back to the bar and bluntly summed it up. 'It's all for the show and to help them spend their money.'

And Mya needed the money. She'd mentioned the tips last night. She could earn more here than on an internship? Even though the internship would progress her career. Brad frowned as he remembered what little he could about her. The girl his parents had been so disapproving of had actually become the Dux of the school—carrying off the elite academic prizes. It had only been because Mya was going to university that Lauren had decided to go too. So surely she was doing as well at university? By rights she should be bonded to some corporate firm already, with a scholarship in return for five years of her working life. Instead she was flinging bourbon around a bar and working back-to-back shifts between the club and a café while squeezing in summer school as well. Something had gone wrong somewhere; the question was, what?

Mya wished Brad would go do his thinking elsewhere. She'd spent all night trying not to think about him, and here he was the minute she'd walked into work. She tried to retain coordination as she checked round the tables making sure all were clean and had the necessary seating arrangements, but she felt his eyes on her.

She'd gone overboard in her reaction to learning he'd

cancelled one of her shifts, but the truth was she couldn't afford to lose a night off work. As it was she worked the bar job and a café job in the daytime. But it wasn't just a silver spoon that Brad had been born with; it was a whole canteen of cutlery. He might work, but it wasn't because he needed the money. He had no idea what it was like for people on the wrong side of the poverty line. And he was so used to getting his own way she was now ridden with the urge to argue with every one of his suggestions.

She walked back to the bar. She'd gone uber-efficient when she'd seen him sitting there. It was a way of working off the insane amount of energy she seemed to be imbued with. It didn't help that he was so gorgeous wearing dark jeans, a belt that drew every eye to his lean waist and a red tee so faded it was almost pink—only Brad could put on pink and make it masculine sexy. Pure ladybait.

Eyes locked with his, she reached for the knife to slice more lemons. Her skin sizzled as he openly looked her up and down.

'You never used to dress so monochrome,' he commented thoughtfully.

He remembered that? Mya had never worn normal in the past, but she didn't have the time to make her crazy outfits any more.

'Needs must,' she said briefly. If she didn't have the time to do something properly, she preferred not to do it at all, so all the fun she'd once had in creating something from nothing had been put away. Lauren had never worn the latest in fashion either—another thing that had brought them together back at school. She too turned her back on the consumerism of the day, and together they'd done it with style. Mya knew how to sew. She could turn a rag into something unexpected—deliberately setting out to make a statement with her clothing.

He glanced up and grinned at her. 'Still touchy?'

'I didn't sleep well.' She sliced quickly.

'Nor did I. I kept looking at your picture on my phone.'

She paused, eyes glued to the knife. No way could she dare look at his expression this second. 'I don't want to know what you were doing with my picture.'

'I never looked at you that way before.'

Oh, like that was meant to make her feel better?

'I'm aware of that,' she snapped. 'It was not 'til you saw the bikini.'

'No, I was otherwise occupied. I'm sorry about that in a way. But to be honest it was a good thing. You weren't ready for me then.'

'I'm not now,' she lied, snapping the knife down on the chopping board, ignoring the way the lemon juice stung her burn.

'Oh, you hold your own,' he said. 'And you know it.'

Her phone vibrated against her leg. She frowned and pulled it out. But it wasn't a text; it was a reminder from her calendar.

Oh, no.

'Are you okay? You've changed colour.' Brad raised his voice. 'Mya?' He asked more sharply. 'Bad news?'

She tried to smile but couldn't force the fear far enough off her face to manage it. How *could* she have made such a mistake? She had everything on file, had due dates highlighted *and* underlined, but she'd been too busy dreaming up exotic cocktails and daft names to christen them in the past twenty-four hours to check. In other words, she'd been having too much *fun*.

She'd been so distracted she'd said yes to the extra

shift at the café when they'd called last minute, forget-
ting to check her diary just in case. She'd figured it was
better to keep fully occupied and thus ward off danger-
ous, idle-moment thoughts. Brad-type thoughts and re-
plays of an unexpected, crazy kiss. She'd been distracted
by imaginary conversations with a guy. About a *party*?

As a result, the assignment due tomorrow for her
summer course had slipped her mind. She'd not done it.
She'd not even *half* done it. She hadn't done nearly the
amount of research and reading she should have. She
was playing everything close to the wire at the moment,
every minute screwed down to either work or study, and
last-minute deadlines had become the norm in recent
weeks—so long as she had the info she needed. Mya
was good enough to wing it. But just winging it wasn't
good enough for her. She wanted to ace it. She wanted
her perfect GPA back. She wanted her perfect control
back. She didn't want to be sleepless and thinking saucy
thoughts at inappropriate hours of the day. She was *such*
a fool to let herself be distracted. Especially by Brad
Davenport. She drew a deep breath into her crushed
lungs. No more distraction.

'Nothing I can't manage,' she lied and brought the
bottles back to the line-up of shot glasses to pour more
cherry-cheesecake shots for the trio of babes at a nearby
table who were wearing 'so hot right now' dresses and
drinking in the vision of killer-in-casual Brad.

'Really?' He watched her with absolute focus, as if
he had no idea that he'd caught the undying attention of
every woman in the building. But he knew it already—
it was normal for him.

She nodded and looked down to concentrate on pouring the vodka in the glasses, not trusting herself to speak
again without snapping at him. Suddenly she was too

stressed to be company for anyone, and his utterly innate gorgeousness irked her more than was reasonable.

He put both palms on the bar and leaned closer. 'Mya?'

That underlying note of concern in his deep voice didn't help her combat the melting effect his mere presence had on her bones. His observation of her made her butter-fingered—not good when she had to flip two glass bottles at once in performing-seal fashion. Smashing the spirits would see the dollars coming out of her pay packet. 'I need to concentrate.' She offered a vaguely apologetic smile. 'We'll have to talk about the party later.'

'Sure.' He eased back and flashed her a smile that would easily have coaxed her own out had she looked long enough.

But she resolutely kept her eyes on the glasses as she fixed the cranberry layer in them, because she was not allowing him to distract her any more. She put the shots onto a tray, lifted it and slowly walked out from behind the bar, to carry them to the divas. They were all looking over her shoulder, checking out Brad.

'You know him?' one of them asked in an overly loud whisper as Mya put the tray on the table between them. 'He's single?'

'Permanently,' Mya answered honestly. She glanced around and saw he hadn't moved. Worse he had a smile on, not his usual full-strength-flirt one, but a small twist to the lips that somehow made him even *more* attractive. It was so unfair the way he could make hearts seize with a mere look. She turned back to the pretty women. 'But he loves to play.'

And no doubt he'd adore three women at once. Maybe if she were to see him go off with the trio for some de-

bauched night, then she'd blast away the resurgence of
this stupid teen crush and be able to concentrate wholly
on the wretched assignment she had ahead of her.

One of the girls stood and went over to talk to him.
Mya went straight back behind the bar and tried not to
pay attention to the high-pitched laughter. But she knew
it was exactly two and a half minutes until he joined the
women at their table. Mya decided to let Jonny serve
them from then on.

She ignored the way the women leaned forward and
chatted so animatedly. She ignored the laughter and
smiles that Brad gave each of them. Most of all she ignored the way he tried to catch her eye when she walked
past a couple of times. Peripheral vision let her know he
looked up and over to her; she refused to look back. She
had far more important things to think on. And then she
was simply far too busy. People began pouring in as the
sun went down but the night warmed up.

'Jonny, if I don't take my break now, I'm going to miss
it altogether.' She leaned across to beg him.

'Go now.' He nodded. 'Pete and I can handle it.'

She grabbed the oversized ancient laptop she always
lugged round in her satchel all day and took it out to
the small balcony Brad had led her to the other night.
She didn't really know why she'd brought it with her—
it wasn't as if she'd somehow type on her feet as she
worked her shifts at the café and then the bar.

Her heart sank as she scrolled to the relevant docu-
ment. The cases were all cited, but she'd have to try to
get copies of them to read them in full. What library
was going to be open at midnight? She didn't have the
Internet in her small flat as she couldn't afford the connection. She didn't even have a landline. She'd have to
go to a twenty-four-hour café with wireless access and

try to do it from there. Downloading fifteen cases? Oh, she was screwed.

She'd hardly started the first paragraph when Drew came out and caught her hunched over at a corner table.

'You can't sit there studying. This is a bar, not a library,' he grumbled. 'It's not the right look.'

It was the last thing she needed—her control-freak, this-place-must-maintain-its-cool-image boss coming down on her.

'It's my break—surely I can read?' She looked up at him. Didn't he get how desperate she was?

'Not there, you can't,' Drew informed her coolly.

To her horror, tears were a mere blink away. She shut her laptop and stood. Swatting up screeds of legalese in the dark alley outside didn't inspire her but if that was what she had to do, she'd do it. It was going to be an all nighter anyway. Followed by the brunch shift at the café tomorrow. How could she have screwed everything up—*again*?

She walked out past the queue forming at the door and into the night, desperate despite the fact she'd only have a few minutes at most before Drew hunted her out. While the summer sun's heat still warmed the air, it was now dark. Hooray for the safety torch on her keychain; she'd be able to read the fine-print text on the step at the back entrance of the bar.

'Big essay?' Brad had followed her, gazing at the ancient computer in her hand.

She nodded glumly, her stomach knotting again. 'Due tomorrow and I've not done it and I don't have half the case law I need,' she confessed.

'Tomorrow?'

She winced. Did he have to hammer home her incompetence? 'I need to read up.' In other words, she needed him to go back inside and keep chatting to those women.

'How long's your break?'

'Twenty minutes.'

'You can't possibly concentrate here.' He frowned at the giant recycling bin into which they threw all the empty bottles. Yeah, the sound of smashing glass was regular and went well with that thudding bass beat coming through the brick walls of the converted warehouse.

'I can concentrate anywhere.' If she had the info she needed.

'And do an assignment in twenty minutes? You might be brilliant, Mya, but you're not a magician.' He frowned. 'How come you don't have the case law?'

'I did an extra shift at the café today,' she said. 'I forgot about the assignment.'

'You have too much on.'

'Yes, so I need to work now,' she said pointedly. But he didn't take the hint. Instead he cocked his head and came over all thoughtful.

'I've got access to all the legal databases. Including the subscription ones at my place,' he said.

The ones that cost money to print each article from? The ones that held the case law she hadn't been able to download because she'd done the extra shift at the café? The ones she couldn't get to because the libraries were closed at this time of night?

He pondered another moment. 'Skip your break and ask Jonny to cover the last of your shift. You know he'll do it. He owes you for setting up alone tonight. Come home with me. You can print off all you need and work all night.' He stepped closer, pressing the best point, decisive. 'I'll help you.'

She folded her arms, using her laptop as body armour, mainly to hide the way her thundering heart was threatening to beat its way right out of her chest. 'This isn't a family law assignment.' She tried to play it cool and not collapse in a heap of gratitude at his feet. Or a heap of lustful wishes.

'I covered commercial in my degree too, you know. You're not the only one with dibs on brilliance. I got straight As.'

Of course he did; he was that perfect. And she wasn't. She no longer had the brilliant label at law school. She shook her head. 'I can't cheat.'

'You're not going to,' he growled. Stepping close, he put his hands on her shoulders. 'I'm not going to write the assignment for you,' he said firmly, as if she were a kid who had to have the simplest thing explained to her twenty different ways. 'Consider me your law librarian.'

Mya just stared. Feeling the warmth from his firm hands, and seeing his fit frame up close, she felt as if he were like an ad for all-male capability and virility. He was also the least likely librarian she could ever imagine.

He laughed and stepped closer. 'I used to work in the law library as a student. I'm very good at searches.'

'You *never* worked as a librarian.' That she just didn't believe.

'Okay, library assistant,' he clarified, all humble integrity mixed with that killer charm. 'Great job to have as a student.' His wicked grin bounced back. 'I got to meet all the cute girls, and their names and addresses were all on there on the system already.'

'So you abused your position?' Mya drawled, trying to cover the way she wanted to abuse his closeness now and lean against him.

'You're accusing me of wrongdoing?' He shook her and she nearly stumbled that last step right into his arms.

'How come you're so down on me? All I'm trying to do is offer you a little help.'

She kept her balance. She didn't like having to accept help.

'Just some space and some computer access.' He held out the offer as if it were as innocent as a plate of home-made cookies.

While access to those databases would be awesome, what she really couldn't resist this second was his charm. 'Okay, I really appreciate it,' she breathed out in a rush. 'But I don't want to put you out.'

'You're not putting me out.' He let go of her shoulders and turned to walk back down the alley. 'And I promise I won't bother you.'

He didn't have to *do* anything to bother her. He only had to exist. And the nearer he was, the worse it was. But she was just going to have to control that silly part of her body because she had an essay to write.

'Relax and go finish your shift,' he said, leading her past the queue and back into the crowded bar. 'You'll get the info you need and you've got all night to nail it.'

Yeah, but it wasn't the assignment she was thinking of nailing.

CHAPTER FIVE

As Mya went back to mixing concoctions behind the bar, she surreptitiously watched Brad head back to the three beautiful women. Okay, so he was just helping her out with her schoolwork. There was nothing more to his offer. That was fine, perfect in fact. Then a couple of his mates turned up and he introduced the babes to them. Then—Mya couldn't help but notice—Brad stepped back from the conversation. And every time she glanced over—purely to see if their glasses needed refilling, of course—he was watching her. Time and time again their gazes met. And the thing was, he wasn't even giving her the full maple-syrup look, but it had the same effect anyway.

Yeah, she still wasn't over the fact that he was the hottest man she'd ever laid eyes on. It seemed there was a part of her that would always want him, no matter what else she had going on or how much of a player he was.

And had he made the computer-access offer to win her over and into his bed? Possibly. Did that matter? Not really. Because she wouldn't be sleeping in his bed. She'd be getting her assignment written.

It was just before 1:00 a.m. before she could get away—early, as Brad had suggested. Brad's two mates and the three babes had already left the bar, so he was waiting alone, having swapped from drinking beer to soda water hours ago. He straightened from the wall he was leaning against as she neared, her heavy satchel over her shoulder.

'Your place is really only a few minutes away?' she asked, determined to stay matter-of-fact and not crawl up against him and beg him to take her to bed and have his wicked way with her so she'd mindlessly fall into sleep the way she ached to.

He nodded.

Sure enough, just down the road and around the corner from the row of eclectic shops and bars in the more 'alternative' area of town was a street of small, old villas. Every single one of them had been stylishly renovated and looked gorgeous and no doubt cost a mint.

'Why do you live here?' It was nothing like the exclusive suburb in which he'd grown up with the massive modern houses and immaculate lawns.

'I like the mix in the neighbourhood.' He shrugged. 'Lots of good restaurants nearby and it's central.'

'You don't cook?'

'Not often,' he admitted with a flash of a smile.

She waited by the potted rosebush on the wooden veranda while he unlocked the villa and put in the code for the security system. And she knew he was wrong. She couldn't possibly concentrate here, not with him around.

'Let me give you the tour,' he said as he led her the length of the wooden-floored hallway.

'I don't need to see your private things.' She regretted this now. She'd have been better off winging the assignment by cobbling together an average essay with reference to just the few textbooks she had in her flat.

'Yes, you do. Otherwise you'll be curious, and if you're curious you won't be able to concentrate.'

She managed a smile. 'Because all women are curious about seeing your room?'

'Of course,' he said. 'Kitchen and lounge are this way.'

They faced out to the back of the house, the garden not visible this time of night. For a guy who didn't cook, he still had all the mod cons in the kitchen. She stayed in the doorway, really not wanting to take in the atmosphere of being in his personal space.

'Guest bathroom this way.' He brushed past her as he stepped back out to the hall and opened a door on the other side of it. 'Then there are a couple of spare bedrooms. One is my office. The other is a library and workroom for my assistant.' He opened the door opposite.

She didn't go into his office but into the one he'd said was the library. She wouldn't have guessed he'd have a library—certainly not such a varied one.

'You have a whole bookcase of children's books.' She read the spines. She recognised so many she'd read in her hanging-out-at-the-library days when she'd avoided all the other students. Avoided the teasing. That was where she'd met Lauren—who'd been ripping a page out of a book she could have afforded a million times over.

'I work for children,' he answered briefly. 'I got a bulk lot from a second-hand store.'

Internally she laughed at the way everything was shelved in the 'right' place. Clearly he hadn't been kidding about his library-assistant job. She pulled one from the 'teen-read' shelf and flicked it open. Inside the front cover a name had been written in boyish scrawl—Brad Davenport. Second-hand store, huh?

She smiled. 'That was my favourite for years. I read it so many times.'

'Uh-huh.' He took the book off her.

'Did you cry at the end?' she asked.

He smiled but didn't confess.

'I did every time,' she admitted with a whisper.

Still he didn't give it up.

'You don't want me to know that you're a marsh-mallow inside?'

'I'm no marshmallow,' he answered. 'I have them here for the look of it. Generally the kids only come here to meet and talk with me so they're not so nervous in court. I'm not their counsellor or anything. I'm merely their legal representative.'

'But they're your books.' And the kids he was sup-posedly not that close to drew pictures for him that he put on his walls?

His reluctant smile came with a small sigh. 'I like to read.'

'And you like kids?

'Sometimes.' He drew the word out, his voice ring-ing with caveats. 'But I have no interest in having any myself.' He put the book back. 'There are enough out there who've been done over by their dipstick parents.'

'You think you'd be a dipstick parent?'

'Undoubtedly.'

She smiled.

'I think parenting is one of those things you learn from the example you had,' he said lightly. 'I didn't have a great example.'

'So you know what not to do.'

He shook his head. 'It's never that simple. I see the cycle of dysfunctional families in my office every day. Now—' he moved back out of the room '—the last room is my bedroom.'

Mya hovered in the doorway, really not wanting to intrude as the sense of intimacy built between them.

He turned and saw her hesitating and rolled his eyes. 'I promise not to pounce.'

She stepped right into the room. He had the biggest bed she'd ever seen, smothered in white coverings. It would be like resting in a bowl of whipped cream. Definitely not a bed for pyjamas; there should be nothing but bare skin in that.

'Why is it so high?' she asked, then quickly cleared her throat of the embarrassing rasp that had roughened her voice.

'I'm tall.'

'You wouldn't want to fall out of it, would you?' If she sat on the edge of it, her feet couldn't touch the floor. 'It's like Mount Olympus or something.'

There was no giant TV screen on a table at the foot of the bed. No chest of drawers for clothing. No bookshelf. No, it was just that massive bed with the billowing white covering demanding her attention.

'Nice to know I inspire you to think of Greek gods.'

She sent him a baleful look. It was unfair of him to start with the teasing again when she had a whole night of work ahead of her. She was tense enough with unwanted yearning. But she couldn't resist pulling his string a touch—wishing she really could. 'What do I inspire you to think of?'

His gaze shifted to the left of her—to that bed. 'Better not say.'

'Don't tell me you're shy?' She laughed.

'I don't want to embarrass you.'

Oh, it was way too late for that. 'I mistakenly sent you a picture of myself in a half-see-through bikini. I don't think I could be more embarrassed.'

'That was just an image. I couldn't touch you.'

Her breathing faltered, her pulse skipped quicker at

the thought of where and how he was thinking of touching her. And when. Now? Mere words banished the chill she'd felt before as heat crept up her cheeks and across her entire body.

A half-smile curved his lips. 'You like a little talk, don't you? For a woman who's planning to spend the rest of her life counting beans, you have to get your thrills somewhere, huh?'

'There's nothing wrong with chasing financial security.' She chose to ignore the suggestion she might like a little sauce talk.

'Strikes me you chase all-over safety. Which isn't something I can give you,' he warned, leaning close. 'You're not entirely safe with me.'

'Now you tell me, when you've got me alone in your house.' Her insides were melting—that part of her had no desire to be safe right now. It was a dangerous game and one that was so irresistible.

'In the middle of the night.'

She turned and looked at the pretty design on the lower part of the wallpaper. Not just normal wallpaper, but almost a mural. Good diversion. 'The room came like this?'

'No, I chose it.' He let her pull back from the brink.

'You did?' It made the room like a grotto—with that big bed in the middle and the soft-looking white pillows and duvet. 'Okay, you chose it with women in mind.'

'No, I liked my tree house when I was a kid. Remember that?'

She did remember the old hut up high in one of the ancient trees at his parents' house. She and Lauren had been banned from it. It had been padlocked and everything. His escape from the magazine-spread-perfect house. Lauren had got her escape by banning her mother from her room.

'This gives me the same feeling of peace.' He walked towards her. 'And women don't sleep in here.'

Yeah, right. 'Because you have a separate bedroom for your seduction routine? One with boxes of condoms and sex toys?'

'I don't need sex toys,' he boasted with a self-mocking smile. 'And you've already seen the spare rooms. One's my office, one's my library.'

'So what, you're celibate?' She let her eyebrows seek the sky.

'I prefer to sleep-over at their houses. It makes the morning-after escape easier.'

She shook her head but couldn't help the laugh. 'You're bad.'

'No, I'm good. It's easier for both of us. Women tend to be more relaxed in their own environment.'

'Do you even make it to the morning, or do you sneak out while she's still asleep?'

'I never *sneak* out.' He walked a step closer still. 'There's nothing like starting the day with sex. I leave her recovering in bed after that.'

'And dreaming of another encounter that will never happen.' Mya desperately clung to some kind of mockery but all she could think about was kissing him, about starting the day with sex—with him.

'Why ruin a beautiful memory?' He smiled. 'One perfect night is all that's required. More just gets messy.'

She suspected just the one with him would get messy for her. Her one and only one night had been hideous the next day.

'Now,' he said softly, so close in her personal space now her pulse was frantic. 'You can either work in my office or the library. You've got your laptop.' He glanced at the dinosaur beast in her bag. It weighed a ton but still had a word-processing program that worked. That was all that mattered. 'Let's go with my office.' He made the decision for her. 'I'll pull up the cases you need while you get reading. And my computer is faster in there than the one in the office. You can type up your assignment on that—be better for you ergonomically.'

Mya dragged in a shaky breath, determinedly so *not* disappointed he hadn't kissed her, and followed him to the office.

There was really only one reason why Brad had offered to help Mya. One carnal, driving reason. But now she was in his house he fully regretted it. Her scent tormented him. The light sweetness overlaid with the tart lemon from the bar. Yeah, that was Mya. He switched on the computer with deliberately calm movements. In truth, he wanted to spin in his seat and grab her, have her over his desk in a second and kiss every inch of her skin. Here, in his bed, the kitchen, everywhere. He had the sinking feeling she'd haunt his house for ever if he didn't get her out of his system.

But there was no doubt she was waiting for him to make his move. His playboy reputation had all her barriers up, and though he knew he could eventually get her to say yes, he didn't want to be that predictable. He didn't want her thinking she knew all there was to know about him. Because she didn't. He wasn't *that* out of control. He didn't *want* to be that out of control. And he wasn't that shallow—at least he hoped not. So he bit back the raging lust and concentrated on the case searches instead.

He quickly read the list she pulled out. It wouldn't take him that long.

She had her textbook out and was making notes already. He smiled as he watched her discreetly while logging in to the online databases. She was so natural with her hair tied back and her pen in hand, ready to take notes as she read—fast. She'd eased right into it, looking more relaxed and at home than he'd ever seen her in the bar, for all the effort that she put in there. And that was the difference, he figured: there it was a big effort, whereas this—reading, studying, thinking—was effortless for her. And natural.

'You really like corporate law, or is it about the earning potential?' he couldn't resist asking when he was about halfway through the list.

She lifted her head and met his eyes for a too-short moment. 'I really do like it.' She looked at the pages. 'Does that surprise you? I like the challenge. I like figuring out the rules. I like the power in negotiation.'

He nodded but couldn't help thinking she was holding something back. Her drive was so strong.

'You think I'm shallow?' She looked up again and this time he saw the flicker of insecurity in her eyes. It mattered to her what he thought of her?

'No,' he answered honestly. 'Different people enjoy different things. Different people have different things driving them.'

She nodded, but to his disappointment didn't open up more.

'Why are you doing summer school?' He couldn't help asking. 'Why do you work so many shifts? Aren't you on scholarship?'

'Not any more.'

'Why not?'

Mya took in a deep breath. She never usually discussed this—but telling Brad might be a darn good idea. It might help keep her focused around him. 'I failed.'

His fingers stopped on the keyboard and he swivelled in the chair to face her. 'You finally flunked an exam? Don't worry about it—everyone does sometime.'

Somehow she didn't think he had. 'I didn't flunk one. I flunked them all. Finals last year I completely crashed.'

'What happened?' His eyes widened.

Yeah, it had been a shock to her too. She'd always been the super-bright one. The rebellious but diligent student who was there on sufferance because she dragged the school's academic rankings up single-handedly.

'What happened?' he asked again when she said nothing. 'Your family? Is everyone okay?'

'It was nothing catastrophic.' She turned away and began underlining random sentences with pencil. 'It was embarrassing.'

'So what happened?'

She really didn't want to go into it but going into it would put the ice on any hot thoughts—hers and his— and she wanted to get through this night without being tempted. 'I met a guy. I thought he was, you know, the *one*.' Now she was blushing with embarrassment, because she'd been so naïve. 'But he totally wasn't. He broke up with me two days out from exams and I…handled it badly.' It was mortifying now to look back on, but she'd been hurt. She'd finally thought she'd found a place to fit in, and she couldn't have been more wrong.

'What a jerk breaking up at exam time.'

She nodded. 'He was. But I was an idiot. A big idiot.' Because she'd gone out and made everything worse.

'How big?'

'I went out and got really drunk.'

'Oh.' He was silent a moment. 'Did something bad happen?'

'Not bad. But not that great either.' She glanced at him. 'My own mistake and I've learned from it.' The responsibility lay with her. She was the one who'd lain in bed crying her eyes out. She was the one who'd gone out and got drunk to try to forget about him and ease the pain. She was the one who'd brought home some random guy and slept with him just to feel wanted. She'd woken up the morning of her first exam with a dry mouth and a sick stomach and an inability to remember the name of the man in her bed. She'd been mortified and ashamed and sick. Hung-over and bleary-eyed, she'd not even made it past the first hour of the exam. The one that afternoon she'd turned up, signed her name and walked out again. The last exam she'd actually tried to do something on but had panicked halfway through and walked out. Her supervisor had called her in when the results came out. Had asked what had happened, had wanted her to get a doctor's note or something because her performance was so shockingly below her usual standard. Below anyone's standards. But she could never have done that. It was her fault, her responsibility.

She'd fed from the scholarship fund long enough. All her secondary schooling, now half her university degree. No more. She was making her own way in the world—and paying her own way. Nothing mattered more than gaining financial independence, by getting a good job. And if it meant it took longer for her to finish her degree working part-time, so she could live, then that was just the way it had to be.

'What have you learned?' Brad asked.

She turned and looked at him directly. 'That I can't let

anything or anyone get in the way of my studies again. Definitely no man, no relationship.

'That's why you don't want to get involved with anyone? That's why it's inconvenient?'

'That's right.' She nodded, denying the other reason even to herself. 'I'm busy. I'm working at the bar every night and at the café on the weekends. I've got lectures midweek and assignments and reading to do in and around that. I just don't have time for anyone or anything else.'

'You can't let one bad experience put you off for ever.'

'Not for ever. Just the next couple of years.'

He frowned. 'But you get time off over Christmas, right?'

'From lectures but I have assignments and I have shifts right the way through.' The public holidays paid good money, and patrons were more generous tippers too. 'I'm not interested in anything.'

'Not a great quality of life for you, though, is it? All work and no play.'

'It's not for ever,' she said again.

'No? How many years are you off finishing your degree?'

'Part-time it's going to take me three. That's with taking summer papers as well.'

'So no nookie for you for another three years?' He shook his head, looking appalled. 'That's more than a little tragic.'

'Sex isn't the be-all and end-all,' she said with more confidence than she felt.

'It's up there. Without sex there can be no life.'

'We're not talking biology here.'

'You're going to be miserable,' he warned.

'I'm not. I'm going to achieve what I want to achieve.'

'With no help from anybody.'

'You understand, right?'

'No, I don't.'

Startled, she looked at him.

'I don't see why it has to be that miserable.' He turned and met her eyes. 'No such thing as balance with you, is there?'

'I have to do what I have to do. And I'm not into the casual-sex scene.' She cleared her throat, trying to hold the blush at bay as she remembered that mortifying morning. 'I learned that too. I don't want a fling. But nor do I want a relationship right now. I have too much else to do.'

'All or nothing,' he murmured.

'Right now it's nothing,' she confirmed.

He looked at her, brown eyes serious. 'Okay.' He held her gaze. 'Message received loud and clear.'

She said nothing. He turned back to the computer and pulled the list of cases nearer. Mya watched his fingers fly over the keyboard. Serious, focused.

That was it? She'd told him as explicitly as she could that she didn't want an affair and he just accepted it?

Because here was the thing—she was still totally hot for the guy. How could he be so focused when she was dying of desire? She'd gone for honesty and he'd taken it. He'd backed right off. But instead of feeling any kind of relief, she felt *more* wound up. She'd been so sure he'd make some kind of move. She'd been so sure she'd say no. Only there were no moves from him, and only *yeses* and *pleases* circling in her head.

She couldn't believe her madness. Her brain had been lost somewhere between here and the bar.

He stood and picked up the pages as they came out of the printer and put highlighters and sticky notes in front of her. She almost laughed. It seemed the guy was as much of a stationery addict as she was.

'It's all vital for doing an assignment.' He winked. 'I'm off to make you some coffee while you get started.'

He'd left the documents open on screen so she could cut and paste quotes as necessary. Hell, he'd even opened up a documents file, named for her, and saved the other cases he'd downloaded. She stared at them, not taking in a word, just waiting.

Five minutes later he put the steaming mug in front of her and stayed on the other side of the desk.

'I'm turning in now. There's more coffee in the machine in the kitchen, fruit in the bowl, chocolate on hand too. Stay as late as you like. Don't go walking out there at some stupid hour of the morning.'

'I can't stay the whole night.' There was just no way.

'It'll probably take you all night to get the assignment done anyway. No point in taking unnecessary risks.' He walked back to the doorway in jeans and tee—she noticed his feet were now bare.

'Thanks,' she said rustily. 'Really appreciate this.' And was so disappointed when he disappeared down the hallway.

She stared at the screen. All this info was at her fingertips. All she had to do was read, assimilate, process, write. It wasn't that hard. She'd done enough essays to know what her lecturers wanted and what it was she needed to get that extra half grade.

But the house was silent.

Acutely aware of his presence under the roof, she sat stupidly still, listening for sounds of him. Imagining going to find him—imagining sliding into that mountainous cloud of a bed and...

She'd pushed him away and it had worked. For *him*.

She still wanted what she couldn't have and with that she'd lost her ability to concentrate. That was a first. She glanced at the big printer on the table behind her. Half a tree's worth of paper and twenty minutes later she was ready to leave.

'What are you doing?' he asked just as she'd tiptoed to the front door.

She whirled around. What was she doing? What was *he* doing standing there almost completely bare? Only a pair of boxer shorts preserved his modesty and even then they were that knit-cotton variety that clung rather than hung loose. And speaking of things being *hung...*

She burned. 'I can't work here.' It was a pathetic whisper.

'You're sneaking out.' He crossed his arms. It only emphasised his biceps. It was so unfair of him to have such a fit body.

'I didn't want to wake you.'

'How are you planning on getting home?'

'I can walk.'

'It's after two in the morning.'

'I walk home from the bar all the time. I have a safety alarm. I walk along well-lit streets. I'm not stupid.'

His jaw clenched. 'Take my car.'

Could he make it worse for her? 'No, that's okay. I'm fine walking.'

'It's not fine for anyone to walk home alone this time of night. Take my car.'

She sighed. 'That's very kind of you, but I can't.'

'You have a real issue accepting help, don't you?' he growled.

Possibly. Okay, yes, particularly from him. His whole 'friendly' act was confusing her hormones more. 'I can't drive,' she admitted in a low voice. 'I've never got my licence. I've never learned to drive.'

For a second his mouth hung open. 'Everyone learns to drive. It's a life skill. Didn't your dad teach you?'

Her dad didn't drive either. That was because the accident at the factory years ago had left him with a limp and unable to use his right arm. He'd been a sickness beneficiary ever since. Living in a house that was damp, in a hideous part of town that was getting rougher by the day. She was determined to get her parents out of there. She owed it to them. 'You're assuming we had a car,' she said bluntly. They couldn't afford many things most people would consider basic necessities, like a car and petrol or even their power bill most of the time.

'Okay.' He turned and strode back to his bedroom. 'I'll drive you.'

'You don't have to do that,' she called after him, beyond frustrated and embarrassed and frankly miserable.

'Yes, I do.'

'I didn't want to disturb you.'

'It's way too late for that.' He returned, jeans on, tee in hand. 'I'll drop you home.'

She needed him to put the tee on, and she really needed him too. She'd had such sensual thoughts in the past hour she was almost insane with it.

But he read her fierce expression wrong. 'Don't you dare argue with me any more.'

He opened the front door and waited for her.

To her horror her eyes filled and she quickly walked out. She was too strung out to argue. She'd not admitted to anyone the struggle she'd been having. Not even to Lauren. But she was so tired. The relentless shifts, the constant pressure of squeezing in assignment after assignment, of fitting in lectures around work, of desperately trying to get the highest of grades every time, of never, ever getting enough sleep. But it was something she alone had to deal with. And she certainly couldn't lose more time or sleep fantasising about him.

CHAPTER SIX

BRAD's tension didn't ease as he unlocked the car and opened the passenger door in the middle of the night for her. For someone so independent, her inability to drive threw him. They lived in New Zealand. Everyone drove here. And she shouldn't be walking home alone night after night after work at the bar. She was so pale; the amount of work she had on bothered him. It didn't help that he'd lumbered her with this party as well. He was thoughtless. And, yes, selfish.

Because all it had been about was him stealing time with her. He'd wanted her—and any excuse would do to get that time. But now? Now he really was concerned.

'I'll teach you to drive,' he said, putting his car in gear and pulling out into the quiet, dark street.

'Thanks all the same but it's not necessary. I live centrally. I walk to work. I use public transport—it's better for the environment.'

'You're happy to learn bar tricks from Jonny,' he pointed out, annoyance biting at her refusal.

'I wouldn't want to damage your car.'

His body tautened to a ridiculous degree, urging him to pull over and kiss her into silence. Into saying yes— to this, to anything, to *every*thing. He wanted her more than he'd ever wanted a woman. Who'd have thought that a picture could have affected him like this?

No. It wasn't just the picture. It was every time she opened her mouth and shot him down while eating him up with her eyes. If they ever got it on, it would be mind-blowing. He knew it. But that wasn't happening. She wasn't into flings and he wasn't into anything else and he was man enough to back off. He'd drop her home now and go out tomorrow night and find a new friend to play with.

But the idea left him cold. Instead, he went back to thinking about her.

'About Lauren's party.' He revved the engine while waiting at another infernal red light. The ten-minute drive seemed to be taking for ever. 'If it's too much for you—'

'It's not too much.' She interrupted him and he heard the attempted smile in her voice. 'I just got behind on this one assignment and I'll get that done tonight. At home. I want to help. I can do it. Just to the left here is fine.' She pointed out her apartment.

'I haven't thought much more about it.' He hadn't thought about the party at all. He'd spent all his spare moments imagining the delicious things he'd do to Mya the minute she let him.

She turned to face him as he cut the engine. 'The cocktails will be fun. Just get in a good band and a DJ and good food. It'll be fine.'

He flicked on the interior light so he could see her properly. 'You wouldn't be lowering your standards for me, would you?'

The colour ran under her skin but she kept on her smile as she shook her head. 'I'd never do that. I still expect the best.'

Brad grinned despite his disappointment. She'd have got the best. Her automatic, instant refusals of anything he offered? They pricked his pride. He wished she'd come to him, wished she'd be as unable to resist their chemistry as much as he seemed unable to.

'I really don't know how to thank you.' She clutched the door handle, her eyes wide and filled with something he really wished was desire.

'I can think of a couple of ways.' He couldn't help one last little tease.

'You've a one-track mind, haven't you?' she teased right back, but she looked away from him, drawing a veil over that spark.

The devil in him urged to press her for a date, but he already knew her answer. She was either working or studying, every waking minute. So he let her go and drove home in the darkness. But once there he remained wide-awake and restless and *hot*. Nothing was going to happen between them, but that hadn't diminished the ache and the hunger. Lust. He'd get over it. But as he sat in front of his computer, the sky lightened and he got to wondering whether she'd finished her assignment. Whether she was working her shift. Whether she was okay. And then he realised he wasn't going to be able to rest until he knew for sure that she was.

Mya knew that if she could survive tonight, she could survive anything. She showered to refresh her system but it was a bad idea. The warm water made muscles melt and her mind wander into dangerous territory. She flicked the jets to cold. Then she dragged herself to her desk and pulled out the piles of paper and opened her ancient laptop. She had four hours. She didn't have time to lust after anyone.

Finally she got in the zone. She read—fortunately she was fast at it—assimilated, analysed and wrote, fingers thumping the keyboard. Her phone alarm beeped at seven forty-five just as she was finalising the formatting. She packed up and sprinted to the café. There was Internet access there. She grabbed a coffee and hit Send on the email. Her assignment was safely en route to her lecturer's inbox. She straightened and stretched out the kinks in her back from hunching over her keyboard. Exhaustion hit her like a freight train. Only now she had to put on an apron and start making everyone else's coffees.

Two hours later she switched her phone to mute and put it in the cubby so she'd no longer be bothered by the zillion messages she was receiving. Brad had sent the invites to everyone about the same time she'd sent the assignment to her lecturer. She'd never expected he'd follow through so quickly or with such impact. She should have known better. Brad Davenport was all about impact.

She'd been impressed by the slick black-and-white mysterious message that had spread over the screen of her phone when she'd clicked on it. Yeah, she'd been fielding texts and calls all morning with people wanting the inside deal on what the plans were for the party—all excitement and conjecture. Because the Davenports were the ultimate in cool. Stylish, unique and rolling in it, and anyone who was anyone, or who wanted to be someone, wanted this invite. She'd answered honestly that she hadn't a clue what was planned but that they'd better be smart enough to keep it secret from Lauren. Mya had threatened them with a prolonged and agonising social-death sentence should anyone spoil the surprise.

Her shift crawled to its end. She was almost in tears

with relief and at the same time ready to drag herself across town. She'd doze in the bus on the way. The last person she expected to see just outside the café door was Brad.

'What are you doing here?' Was she so tired she was hallucinating?

'I thought I'd give you a lift home. You must be exhausted.'

Not a hallucination, he was real. Looking so strong and smiling, and she wished she didn't have any stupid scruples.

'I'm okay.' She was so tired, it was harder to control her reaction to his proximity and the urges he inspired.

'You got it done?'

She nodded, glad he'd reminded her of her work. 'Thanks for coming in but I'm not going home. I'm having lunch with my parents.' She was due there this minute.

'I'll give you a ride.'

'No, it's fine,' she hurriedly refused. 'I take the bus.'

He looked at her. 'I can give you a ride.'

'Shouldn't you be working?' She really didn't want him taking her there.

'I'm due a lunch break too.'

'But—'

'Can you stop saying no to me in everything?' he asked. 'I'm offering as a *friend*, Mya. Nothing more.'

She opened her mouth and then shut it again as she registered the ragged thread of frustration in his voice. He must be tired too—that invitation would have taken some time on the computer. Had he not slept a wink either?

'You don't have to do this,' she said softly ten minutes

later as they headed towards the motorway that would take them right across town and to the outskirts.

'Don't worry, I won't embarrass you.' He reached over and gave her knee a teasing squeeze. 'I won't tell them you like sending people racy pictures of yourself.'

She managed a light laugh but her discomfort mushroomed as she realised he was going to see the worst.

'Are *you* embarrassed?' he asked quietly. 'You don't want me to see your home?'

'No,' she argued instantly. 'But you wouldn't be the first person to look down your nose at my neighbourhood. We come from totally different worlds, so don't act like you're all understanding and down with it. You can't ever relate.'

'Your shoulders aren't broad enough for a chip this big.'

'Oh, it's a chip, is it? It's just me being oversensitive?' She twisted in her seat to face him. 'What would you know? Have you ever faced the judgments and expectations from each side of the economic divide? Girls from the wrong side of the tracks like me are only good for a fling.' Never marriage material. That was how James had treated her. At first he hadn't known. He'd been attracted to her academic success, but when he'd found out about her background, he'd run a mile. 'All *you've* ever wanted from women like me is sex.'

'All I've ever wanted from *any* woman is sex,' he pointed out lazily. 'It has nothing to do with your family background.'

About to launch into more of a rant, she stopped and mentally replayed what he'd said. And then she laughed.

'I mean really—' he winked '—you don't think you're taking this too seriously? We're in the twenty-first century, not feudal England.'

She shook her head. 'Twenty-first century or not, the class system operates. There's an underclass you know nothing about.'

'Don't patronise me,' he said. 'I'm not ignorant. I'm aware of the unemployment figures and I've dealt with worse in my work. You've got no idea of the dysfunction I see. I can tell you it crosses all socioeconomic boundaries. Sometimes the worst are the ones who have the most.'

'Yeah, but you don't know the stress financial problems can bring.'

'That's true. I don't have personal experience of that. But I'm not totally without empathy.'

'And salary doesn't necessarily equate with effort,' she grumped. Her mother worked so hard and still earned a pittance. That was why she'd insisted Mya study so hard at school, so she'd end up with a job that actually paid well. And Mya wanted to work to help her parents.

'Mya.' He silenced her. 'I know this might amaze you, but I'm not that stupid or that insensitive.'

She put her head in her hands. Of course he wasn't. 'Sorry.'

She heard his chuckle and let his hand rub her shoulder gently—too briefly.

'I'll let you away with it because I know how tired you are,' he said.

But her discomfort grew as they neared. He'd been right—she didn't want him seeing it. She was embarrassed. Embarrassed she hadn't done something sooner to get her parents out of there. She should have done so much more already. 'You can just drop me, okay?'

'Sure,' he answered calmly. 'They must be impressed with how hard you're working at the moment.'

Mya chewed her lower lip. 'They don't know.'

'Don't know what?'

'Don't know anything.'

'That you work at the bar, the café or that you're not at uni full-time?'

She shook her head. 'They don't know I lost the scholarships. They don't know I'm at summer school. They can't know. Can't ever.' She felt tears sting. Stupid tears—only because she was tired.

He took his eyes from the road for too long to stare at her. 'And you're that stressed about them finding out?'

'Of course I am. Watch the traffic, will you?'

He turned back to stare at the road, a frown pulling his brows. 'I think you should tell them.'

Her breath failed. 'I can't tell them. They're so proud of me. It's...everything.'

'They'd understand.'

They wouldn't. She'd be a failure. She didn't ever want to let them down. She didn't want disappointment to stamp out the light in their eyes when they looked at her. 'You don't get it. I'm the only one to have even finished school. They're so proud of me, they tell everyone. I can't let them down now. This is what I am to them.' It was all she was.

'Everyone stuffs up sometimes, Mya. I think they'd understand.'

'They wouldn't. And I couldn't bear for them to know. It alienated me from the others. My cousins, the other neighbourhood kids... They gave me a hard time then. I don't want more of a hard time now. I don't want my parents disappointed. Life's been tough enough on them.'

She'd been bullied as she walked across the neighbourhood in her school uniform—the only kid in the block to go to a school with a uniform. Taunted—told she'd become a snob, torn down. *Freak. You think you're better than us?*

She hadn't thought that. She knew just how hard those in her 'hood worked—or worked to try to get a job. Sure, a couple hadn't. A couple had gone off the rails in the way Lauren had once threatened to. But she knew better than anyone that snobbery worked both ways. In the one hand she'd carried the hopes and dreams of her parents; in the other she'd been burdened with the spite and jealousy of others. She didn't fit in here any more, but she sure hadn't fitted in with her new school either.

And now she was held up as the neighbourhood example—her cousin's five-year-old daughter had said she wanted to go to uni and be just like her. She couldn't let them down.

She'd had opportunities others hadn't had and she'd squandered them on a man who was so removed from her own sphere—that elite, born-to-it world that she'd never once felt comfortable in. She couldn't let them know what an idiot she'd been. And she couldn't be that naïve girl again. This damsel was doing her own rescuing. No man, no fairy-tale fantasy, would come between her and her studies.

'How will you get home after lunch?' he asked as they neared her home.

'Same as always.'

She knew he was looking at the gang symbols graffitied on the fences they passed. The lush greenery of the affluent central suburbs gave way to unkempt, sunburned brown grass and bare dirt. The old-looking swing-set in the park and the new activity set that had already been defaced, litter spilling from the bin. She knew what he was thinking; she thought it too. The neighbourhood wasn't just rough; it was unsafe and was worsening. Her resolve firmed. She was getting her parents out of here as soon as she could.

They were sitting on the porch when Brad turned into the driveway. The two-bedroom government-supplied house had been modified so her father could walk in easily. He didn't rise as Brad stopped the car, but her mother hurried over. Brad got out of the car and greeted her with his intensely annoying polite manners. Mya watched her mother blink a couple of times, watched his full impact on her—that overpowering charm. And she helplessly watched him accept her mother's invitation to join them at lunch. All done before she'd even said hello.

When Brad walked into the house, he was shocked—but not for the reasons Mya might have thought he might be. He'd seen way smaller, emptier properties. No, what shocked him was the wall in the lounge.

It was smothered in the evidence of Mya's achievements. There were certificates everywhere. Certificates going back more than a decade—from when she won spelling competitions at age six. Competitions far beyond her years at that. There were newspaper articles citing her academic successes. There were pictures of her in her uniform. Pictures of her accepting cups and prize-giving. But there were no pictures of her playing.

Proof of their pride in her was everywhere and he realised she hadn't been kidding about the pressure. No wonder her identity was so bound up in performance—*perfect* performance. But surely her parents weren't so success-obsessed for her that they'd disown her if they knew she'd failed? She was their only child.

'Brad's a lawyer. A tutor at university.' Mya walked in with her father, who was leaning on her arm.. 'He's been helping me with my studies this year. He just gave

me a ride because I was running late to get here.' She
bit her lip and looked at Brad as if worried she'd made
a slip in mentioning law school given she was supposed
to be on holiday.

'She doesn't need my help, you know.' Brad went
with her story with an easy smile. 'She's just trying to
make me feel useful.'

The sad thing was he liked feeling useful to her. Even
if in truth he wasn't.

'She's a genius.' Even as he was saying it, he realised
he was buying into the Mya-brain-box worshipping—
doing it as badly as her parents. Talking her up until she
was terrified of failing. Mya, who needed no help academically because she was such a star. Never-fail Mya.
Never *dare* fail.

So he switched. 'But she works really hard at it.'

He encountered a beseeching green gaze just at the
moment her mother's proud tones came from the other
side of the table.

'Mya always works hard.'

Brad worked hard himself then, keeping the conversation light—and away from work. Mya was abnormally
quiet and giving him keen looks every so often. It bothered him she was so nervous—what did she think would
happen? Did she trust him so little? He wouldn't let her
down and give her away.

'I hope it wasn't too bad my staying.' He finally apol-
ogised for butting in when they were back in his car and
driving towards town. 'But I really enjoyed it.'

'It was hardly your usual restaurant standard,' she
answered brusquely.

'You couldn't get fresher than that salad,' he pointed
out.

That drew a small smile. 'It's the one thing he likes

the most but tending the garden takes him a long time. He has chronic pain and he gets tired.'

'It was an accident?'

'In the factory years ago.' She nodded. 'He's been on a sickness benefit since. Mum does the midnight shift at the local supermarket.' She sighed. 'So now you know why I want to get the big corporate job.'

He nodded.

'I want to move them somewhere else. Somewhere much nicer.'

'I can understand that.' He paused. 'You really care about what they think of you, huh?'

'Don't you care about what your folks think of you?'

He laughed beneath his breath. 'It no longer matters to me what either of them think.'

'No longer? So it used to?'

'When I was a kid I wanted to please Dad.' He laughed—the small kind of laugh designed to cover up real feelings.

Mya didn't want him to cover up. 'But you don't any more?'

'I'm really good at my job and I enjoy it. What he thinks is irrelevant.'

'What did he do?'

'He didn't do anything.'

'I'm not stupid either, Brad.' She turned in her seat to study his profile directly.

'So you know what he does.' Brad trod harder on the accelerator and gave her the briefest of glances. His warm brown eyes now hard and matte. 'Buys his way out of anything.'

'What did he buy his way out of for you?' Mya asked quietly.

Attention. It was all about attention. For him. For

Lauren. He'd once asked his father to come and see him in a debating contest of all things. Sure, not the most exciting of events, but he'd been fifteen years old and still young enough to want his father's approval. At that time he'd wanted to *be* his father. A brilliant lawyer, top-earning partner in his firm with the beautiful wife, the yacht, the two kids and the dog.

'I caught him.' Brad surprised himself by answering honestly.

'Doing what?'

'Betraying us.' He glanced at Mya. She'd revealed a part of her life that she preferred to keep private and that she wanted to fix. He wanted her to know that he understood that. So he told her. 'I wanted him to come to see me in the debating final when I was a teen. But he said he had an important meeting he couldn't get out of. I won and went up to show him the medal.' He'd gone up to his father's office, excited with the winning medal in hand, anticipating how he'd quietly hold it up and get the smile, the accolade. Instead he'd discovered that the very important meeting his father hadn't been able to wriggle out of had been with one of the junior lawyers. Fresh from law school, whether she was overly ambitious or being taken advantage of, Brad didn't know and no longer cared.

'The meeting was with a trainee,' he said. 'She was on her knees in front of him.'

'Oh, Brad.'

His father had winked. Winked and put his finger to his lips, as if Brad was old enough—'man' enough—to understand and keep his sordid secret. His scheduled screw more important than his own son. And the promises he'd made to his wife.

So many dreams had shattered that day.

The anger had burned like acid as he'd run home and hidden in the damn tree hut that he hadn't built with his father, but that his father had paid some builder to put in for the look of it.

Brad decided never to be a lawyer like his father. It would never be a father-and-son firm as his father had always envisaged. No insanely high billing rates for Brad. He'd turned to the far poorer-paying child advocacy in direct retaliation to his father. He had the trust fund from his grandfather. He was never going to be short of money. So there was something more worthwhile that he could do. Something that would irritate his accolade- and image-driven dad.

But eventually he realised his father really didn't give a damn what he did. Brad just wasn't that important to him. His gestures might be grand, but they were empty. Just purchases. There was a missing element—no true paternal love. All his father was, was hungry for success, money and women—and for maintaining that façade of the perfect family in society.

'I thought Mother didn't know,' Brad scoffed lightly. 'I thought I was protecting her.' Brad had kept that bitter secret for months, feeling all kinds of betrayal—for himself, his sister and his mother.

'But she did,' Mya said.

He nodded. 'We have an annual barbecue at home for all Dad's staff. And that trainee turned up all confidence and Mother greeted her *so* politely. So knowingly. Coolly making it clear to her that while Dad might screw the secretaries, he'd never leave his wife.'

His mother was as selfish as his father. She wanted what she wanted and was happy to put up with the inconvenience of having a faithless husband. Money and status mattered more than truth. She was so busy pro-

jecting the perfect image. That was the moment that
Brad decided not to help her project that image any more.
That was when he removed himself from home as much
as possible. He'd gone off and found his own fun—with
his own rules.

He looked at Mya. He'd never told anyone that. Not
anyone. Had lack of sleep got to him too? And, yeah, he
regretted mentioning any of it now he saw what looked
like pity in her eyes. He didn't want pity, thanks very
much; he had it all under control. He was more than
happy with the way he managed his life.

'I'm never going to marry,' he said firmly. 'I'm not
going to lie the way they both do.'

'You don't think a long-term relationship can work?'

'Not for me.'

'You're not willing to take the risk?'

'Why would I? I can get all I want.' He smiled, acting
up the playboy answer again. And he figured the women
in his life got what they wanted too. Which wasn't really *him* but the things he could give them—good sex,
fancy dinners, a flash lifestyle. And fun. 'I care about
my work. I like to have fun. I like my space. I like it
uncomplicated.'

'Easy.'

'Is that so wrong?'

'No,' she said softly. 'Not if that's what both parties
want. And understand.'

He trod on the brake and turned to look at her. 'I
don't do relationships, Mya. I do fun and flings and
nothing more.'

'Message received loud and clear.' She echoed his
words of the night before, calmly meeting his stare.

He felt sorry, tired, resigned. 'So this…chemistry between us,' he said slowly.

'Goes nowhere,' she answered. 'It's just one of those things, you know—the friend's older brother...'

'The sister's best friend.'

'We're such a cliché,' Mya acknowledged with a lift of her shoulders. He'd have believed she was amused had her laugh not cracked at the end. 'We've seen too many movies. And you know how it is—you always want what you can't have.'

'We'll be friends.' He did want to remain in contact with her.

She hesitated. Too long for his liking. 'We'll do this party for Lauren.'

And after that? Back to zero contact? It would be for the best. But it wasn't what he wanted at all. He still wanted her to the point of distraction. He'd just have to get over it. Another woman maybe?

He gripped the steering wheel with psycho-killer strength. Appalled with her schedule, he dropped her to university for an hour's lecture knowing she then had to go straight back to the bar for another night's shift. Despite the scratchy feeling beneath his eyelids, he found himself driving to his parents' house. He vaguely tried to remember when it was he'd last been there, and failed. But now was a good time. His father would still be at work and his mother would be at some meeting. He avoided both the house and them as much as possible.

'Hello?' he called out just in case as he opened up the door and disarmed the alarm.

No answer. He took the stairs. His and Lauren's rooms were still neat, still as they'd had them when they were growing up. On a separate floor to their parents, at opposite ends of the hallway from each other, with guest rooms and bathrooms in between. The physical distance was nothing on the emotional distance be-

tween the entire family. And though he and Lauren had
grown a little closer as adults, the gap between parents
and children had only widened.

His mother had read a home-organisation book at
some point in one of her obsessive phases, and all their
personal things were stored in crates, neatly stacked and
labelled in the back of their wardrobes. Schoolwork from
decades ago. When was he ever going to go through
that? When would anyone? But it wasn't his room that
he'd come to grab stuff from. It was Lauren's.

Because that photo of Mya at her parents' house had
reminded Brad that, at one stage in her turbulent teen
years, *Lauren* had taken hundreds of photos. For a long
time she'd preferred the magic of the old-style camera
before messing around with digital. The old playroom
had been converted into a darkroom for her, their parents eager to do anything that might hold Lauren's interest in a topic that was actually palatable to them—not
like boys and underage clubbing. It had long since been
converted back into a study but the boxes of prints remained in Lauren's wardrobe.

He sat on her bedroom floor and flicked through
them, his heart thudding harder and harder as he worked
through the piles. Lauren's best friend, the natural model
for Lauren's photographic phase. It had been the two of
them against the world, right? The rebel and the reject—
the kid who'd not been included by anyone at the hell-
ish, snobby school they'd gone to. Except for Lauren.

Though it was subtle, Mya had changed. The planes
of her face had sharpened, those high cheekbones, the
big green eyes were able to hold secrets now. In her
teen years the attitude was obvious. The resentment,
the defensiveness. But so was the joy, effortlessly cap-

tured in every other photo—that pixie smile, the gleam in her eyes.

Often she had a battered library book in her hand. Every other photo it seemed Lauren had snapped while Mya was unaware—and she was so pretty. The ones where she *was* aware were funny. The madness of some of the pictures made him laugh—terrifying teen girls.

He'd gone to university as soon as he turned seventeen and missed much of this part of Lauren's life. It had been a relief to get out of the house. At the time he'd been too selfish to think of his sister. He'd thought she hadn't known but of course she had. He'd discovered that in their tennis sessions. It was the great unacknowledged truth, how unhappy and dysfunctional their perfect family unit really was. The affairs of his father, the obsessive illness of his mother. They all retreated behind the façades they'd chosen for themselves. His father the distant workaholic, his mother the busy do-good wealthy woman, his sister the tearaway who acted out for any kind of attention. What was left for him but the playboy role?

He paused over one photo. Mya in that prom dress. He should have taken a better look at her in it back then. Then again it was probably better that he hadn't.

She was leaning against the wheel of a car, parked on a lawn that looked as if it hadn't seen a mower in a few months with ratty weeds. With broken headlights and the weeds around the wheel, that car was going absolutely nowhere any time soon. Yeah, that'd be the car she hadn't learnt to drive in.

Brad put that picture to the side and shuffled through some more. He thought about taking the whole box home to look through at leisure but that was a step too far into stalker territory. He flicked through the pile more quickly—Mya wearing some mad hat, Mya draped in what looked like an old curtain. Mya in another dress apparently butchered and sewn together. He looked at the commonality in the pictures. Lauren's pictures of Mya in Mya's crazy—brilliant—creations. So many different things and so out there.

He flipped through them, faster and faster. She'd not always worn black. She'd always worn outrageous. Uncaring of what society might think. She'd made them herself, made that massive statement—'here I am, look at me...'

Where had that fearless girl gone?

Why had she turned herself into a shadow? Now in nothing but black, slinking round as if she hoped she couldn't be seen. Why didn't she want to be seen? Where had the crazy fun gone? She'd grown into a pale, worried woman. A woman who worked too damn hard. Brad held the picture and looked at the smiling face, and slowly his own smile returned as it dawned on him.

It wasn't Lauren who needed a party. It was Mya.

CHAPTER SEVEN

BRAD was lost in thought when his sister thumped his shoulder.

'What was that for?' He frowned, rubbing his biceps more from surprise than pain.

'What's wrong with you?' Lauren asked.

'What do you mean?'

'I mean those two women just swished past you with hips and bits wiggling and you didn't even look at them. Plus I almost beat you today, which has never happened in our whole lives.'

Seated at the tennis-club lounge, Brad felt more confused than ever. 'What women?'

Lauren's mouth fell open. 'Are you sick?'

Okay, he had been somewhat distracted this morning. 'I've got a tough case on.' He offered a genuine excuse. Gage Simmons was truanting again and still not speaking to his psychologist, and the idea of his parents coping with a mediation conference was a joke.

'Isn't that even more reason for you to scope out some action?' Lauren said sarcastically. 'That's your usual stress release, isn't it?'

Once upon a time it had been, sure. But he hadn't looked at another woman in days—there was another consuming his brain space. 'Have you seen much of Mya recently?'

'*My* Mya?' Lauren's pretty nose wrinkled. 'Not much. Why?'

'I ran into her recently,' Brad hedged. Seemed Mya hadn't told Lauren about the mis-sent photo. Good.

'Where?'

'At that bar she works at.'

Lauren nodded and sighed. 'She works all the time.'

'Mmm.' Brad knew if he left the space, Lauren would fill it.

'It was her birthday last month and she couldn't even come for a coffee with me, she was so crunched between work and study,' Lauren said.

Bingo.

'Seems a shame for her.' Brad hesitated, unsure of how to put his idea forward without his sister guessing what it was he'd really wanted. 'Your birthday is coming up soon and you'll get your mitts on all your money.' Her trust fund would be released. 'We'll have to have a huge party.'

Lauren shrugged. 'I don't want it.'

'The party or the money?'

'The money,' said Lauren.

Brad paid proper attention to his sister for the first time all morning. 'What do you mean you don't want it?'

'I'm going to give it away.'

'What? Why?'

Lauren shrugged and looked self-conscious. 'I want to make a difference. You make a difference.'

Brad smothered his groan and at the same time felt affection bubble for his scamp of a kid sister. 'It's easier for me to do that when I don't have to worry about how much I earn in my job. I can afford to take on the

pro bono cases, Lauren. I couldn't do that as easily without the trust fund.'

'That's what Mya said too.' Lauren frowned. 'But
look at her, she's so independent.'

'Yeah, but she's not having much fun with it. Life
should include some fun, don't you think?'

'We all know what you mean by that.' Lauren rolled
her eyes and giggled.

'Not just that. Some simple fun too, you know—party
fun.' Brad stretched his legs out under the table. 'What
are we Davenports good at?'

'Not that much.' Lauren sipped her lemonade through
her straw.

Brad raised an eyebrow. 'But we are. We're really
good at putting on a show, right? Let's put on a show
for Mya.'

'Mya?' Lauren breathed in so quickly she choked on
her drink. Coughing, she asked him the dreaded question. 'You're not going to mess with her, are you, Brad?'

He shook his head. 'No.'

'Hmm.' Lauren didn't look convinced. 'She's not as
strong as she seems, you know. She's actually quite vulnerable.'

'Are you telling me to stay away?' Brad managed a
smile.

'Would it make any difference if I did?' Lauren asked
point-blank. 'I just don't think it would end well. Things
don't end all that well for your women, and Mya's had
enough of that.'

'Don't worry.' Brad grinned, though his teeth were
clenched. 'She's like a sister to me.' What did she mean
things didn't end that well for his women? 'And this is
because I have a venue I need to do something with for
a night.'

'A venue?' Lauren leaned forward, and Brad smiled for real this time. Yeah, his sister had always liked a party. 'So what were you thinking?'

'How's this for a plan?'

Mya got used to the random calls and quickly got in the habit of checking her phone for texts every five minutes. They were short queries about the tiniest details that most people would never think of. One thing to be said for Brad, he was thorough. Very thorough.

In the mornings now he came to the café and ordered a coffee. He never stayed more than ten minutes or so, always moved away when she got busy and had to serve someone. She spent the rest of the day looking forward to her shift at the bar.

Because now he turned up there early every night and urged her to do her worst in creating another cocktail or shot before the crowds came in. She loved the challenge and got the giggles over the often awful results. It didn't matter if she made something that tasted hideous. They laughed about it—with him naming them outrageously. His word play had her in hysterics. He made suggestions; she ran with them. Together they came up with some bizarre mixes that actually worked and many, many failures. But with Brad, failing was more fun than not. And while they worked on it in that calm twenty minutes or so before the crowds appeared, they talked.

She admitted more about her parents' troubles and told him about her cousins who lived around the corner. He listened and then, in turn, 'fessed up more about his parents, and occasionally referenced his work. She knew he was incredibly busy; sometimes he came in looking drained but he always switched 'on' as soon as someone spoke to him. But she knew he went back home after their cocktail-mixing session to do more work. It was why he never drank more than a mouthful of whatever they'd mixed. But mostly they laughed—teasing about everything from taste in music and TV shows to sports teams, and swapped stories of wild, fun times with Lauren.

Mya laughed more in those few minutes each day than she had all year. But fun as it was, it was also slowly killing her because her teen dreams were nothing on the adult fantasies she had now about Brad Davenport. He was so attractive, so much fun and yet so serious about the silliest of things for the party. His concern over the finest of details was so attractive.

In days he became a constant in her life—the one person she saw most of aside from her workmates. It was only for a few minutes, but they were the highlight. And then there were all those texts and the never-ending playlist suggestions for the DJ.

Three days before the party, in between her shifts at the café and the bar, Mya was studying at the library. Her phone vibrated with a message from Brad.

Where are you?

She chuckled at over-educated Brad's inability to use any abbreviated text language. She was similarly afflicted. So she texted back her grammatically correct reply and went back to her books.

She didn't know how long it was before she glanced up and saw him standing at the end of the nearest row of books. 'What are you doing here?'

'It's my natural home.' He winked as he walked nearer.

'But you of all people should know you're not allowed food in the library.' She gave the paper bags he was carrying a pointed look.

'No one will see us.' He jerked his head and sneaked down the stacks away from the study tables and well out of range of the librarian's help desk.

'Brad,' she whispered. But in the end there was no choice but to follow, and she'd come over all first-year giggly student in the library in a heartbeat.

In the narrow space, surrounded by thick, bound books, he opened the bag and pulled out a couple of pottles and put them on a gap in the shelves.

'What is this?' she asked, intrigued.

'Chocolate mousse.'

Of course it was; why had she even asked? But she did, and she had to ask the even more obvious. 'You want me to try them?'

'Yes, they come in these cute little cups, see?' he whispered. 'Which do you think, mint or chilli?'

'You are taking this far too seriously.' She shook her head, but licked her lips at the same time. Yum. She took a tiny bit on two teaspoons and tried them. 'They're both really good. I think Lauren would like—'

'Which do *you* like best?' he interrupted, his gaze boring into her.

Mya's skin goosebumped while her innards seared. She'd missed that look these past couple of days—that full-of-awareness-and-forbidden-desires look. She'd thought he'd gone all friendly and party efficient and had forgotten that kiss altogether—or didn't think it was worth anything. Now all she could think of was that kiss and how much it had moved her and that maybe, just maybe, he was thinking of it too.

'Why does it matter what I think?' She didn't have to try to whisper now. Her voice had gone completely husky. 'This is for Lauren, not me.'

'She'll like what you like,' Brad insisted, stepping closer. 'Come on, tell me.'

She'd never had lust-in-the-library fantasies. Until now. And right now, all she wanted was for Brad to kiss her again in this quiet, still space.

'You've gone red,' he said. 'Was the chilli-chocolate too hot?'

'Must have been,' she muttered.

He was looking at her mouth. Could he please stop looking at her mouth? Did she have a huge gob of mousse on her lip? Because he looked as if he wanted to *taste*, and she wanted him to, very much.

Mya had never felt so hot.

But Brad missed her scorching thoughts. 'Mint it is, then.'

She nodded. Just. 'You've really got into this,' she said, trying to pull herself together as he replaced the lids on the pottles and put them back in the bag.

'I've discovered my latent party-planning talent.' The smallest smile quirked his mouth. He glanced at her and caught her staring. 'So you're all set up to bring her?'

'It's all sorted.' Mya nodded. She'd arranged it with Lauren a few days ago. But now that the party was so close, she felt irrationally ill at ease—even unhappy. She'd be glad when it was over, wouldn't she? She wasn't sure any more. But the worse feeling was the jealousy— she was envious of how much effort he'd gone to for his sister. Which was just mean of her.

She walked away from him, hiding from his intent gaze, back out to the table she'd been studying at. Hopefully he'd leave right away. But he didn't. He pulled out the seat next to hers, sat and flipped open his iPad, hooking into the university's wireless network.

How was she supposed to study now? He didn't get

that when he was around, her brain shut down and all she could think of now was lewd behaviour in the library. She coped for less than five minutes and then she spoke without thinking.

'Did you ever get it on in the library in your librarian days?'

He shot her a startled look.

'I mean—' she felt her blush growing '—that'd be the kind of thing you'd have done back then, right?'

She trailed off as his intense look grew. He slowly shook his head.

He hadn't? *Really?* She'd have thought that Mr Slayer like him would have…but no. He hadn't. Nor had she, of course. And now here they were…

Oh, hell, why did that excite her all the more?

She looked at him and decided honesty was the best policy. 'I can't concentrate on my study when you're around,' she mumbled. 'At the bar, the café, it's different. I don't need to think as hard as I do here. But I can't *think* with you…' She trailed off.

He didn't say anything, just looked at her with those penetrating eyes. He hadn't moved in the past ninety seconds. She wasn't sure if he was even still breathing. Mya felt even hotter than before but now there was a huge dose of embarrassment twisted into her inner furnace as well. She'd all but admitted she still fancied him. But the fact was now she fancied him more than ever. And he'd gone all *buddy* on her.

'Maybe it's best if we work out any last-minute plans over the phone or something,' she said quickly, trying to recover. 'It would be easier, don't you think?'

Slowly he blinked and then seemed to see straight through her. 'That's what you want?'

'That would be for the best,' she squeaked.

He remained still for a very long moment, still watching her. And then he whispered, 'What are you going to wear?'

She froze; like his look, his question breached the boundaries from friendly to intimate—but she'd done that herself already. Now she felt she'd plunged off the edge of a cliff and was swimming in darkness. Who knew which direction the safe beach was? 'I'm not sure.'

'Not black,' he said quietly.

'Probably.'

'No,' he muttered. 'Give me that at least.'

'Okay.' Mya could hardly swallow and her skin was doing that hot-and-cold tingly thing again. 'You've done such a great job,' she said softly, aiming for that conversation-closing platitude—that she meant with all her being. 'She's going to be so thrilled.'

'You think?' His smile lanced her heart. 'I hope so.'

Suddenly he stood, not pausing to pack away his gear, just shoving it into his case as he left.

Instantly she felt bereft. But it was for the best. She looked down at the black-and-white text in front of her—the case names and details she had to understand and memorise. She didn't see any of them. She sighed and blinked to refocus. The sooner the party was over, the better.

He didn't text the day of the party. He didn't need to, of course; he had everything planned to the nth degree. But he'd got her thinking. She wanted to get dressed up. Really get dressed up in a way she hadn't in years. *Her* kind of dressing where she'd been as loud and unconventional—deliberate, girly. Everything unexpected. She'd been in the black jeans so long she'd almost forgotten her old style. But she didn't have any money for anything new and had no time to make anything.

Yet there was one dress she could wear. She shied away from the thought—it would be so obvious, wouldn't it? But she could adapt it, she could wear a wrap or a cardigan or something to dress it down a little…she could get away with it. Maybe.

She went to her parents' house and picked it up, smiling to herself throughout the long bus-ride. She realised she was more excited about seeing him than she was about seeing Lauren's reaction to her surprise.

Once dressed, she went to Lauren's as she'd arranged for their 'girly night out'—their first in ages.

'Look at you!' Lauren squealed when she greeted her at her door.

'Ditto.' Mya laughed at how glamorous Lauren looked.

'Where should we go first?' Lauren asked, her eyes sparkling.

'I promised Drew I'd drop something in at the bar. Is it okay if we go there first?' Mya spun her line.

''Course!'

Mya sent the 'we're coming' text as they climbed into the taxi. All the way there she kept up an inane patter about one of her regular café customers—not Brad. Mya's heart thudded as they swept up the steps. Kirk was on the door and he winked as they walked up and he swung the door open for them.

There was a moment of silence. Then a collective scream.

'Surprise!'

The cacophony of almost a hundred people screaming momentarily deafened her, but Mya chuckled. The glitter confetti bucketing down on them might have been a touch OTT but that was all the more fun. She gazed at Lauren for her reaction.

Only then she noticed that Lauren was looking right back at her with a huge grin on. And then she heard the crowd chanting.

'Mya! Mya! Mya!'

'What?' Mya gazed round in confusion.

Then—who knew from where—a gong sounded and they all screamed again in unison.

'Happy Birthday, Mya!'

Mya clapped her hand over her mouth and shook her head.

'This is for you,' Mya tried to tell Lauren.

'Uh-uh.' Lauren shimmied closer with a wicked smile. 'Fooled you. We all fooled you.'

Shocked, Mya stood immobile. She didn't even breathe—only her eyes still functioned, sending images to her brain. And OMG they were all in on it. Jonny was laughing, her varsity mates. Even Drew was grinning. Her fellow baristas from the café were here. They'd all fooled her. They were all here for *her*.

It seemed Lauren had breathed in giggle-gas as she laughed delightedly, putting her arm along Mya's shoulders.

'But it's not my birthday.' Mya's mouth felt as if she'd been at the dentist for a ten-hour procedure and she had all that cotton-gauze stuff still clogging it.

'You never had a birthday party because you were working.' Lauren laughed more. 'So we took matters into our own hands.'

We.

Mya looked into the smiling crowd once more. Her mouth automatically curved into an answering smile even though she was still in shock, still couldn't believe any of this.

Then she saw him. Brad.

And heaven help her he was all in black—black suit, black tie, black shirt. It emphasised his height, his eyes, his aura of simmering sexuality. The tailored tuxedo a perfect foil for her recycled old prom outfit. If they were a couple, they couldn't have planned it better. Except they weren't and they hadn't.

But he'd planned it—this whole party. Had it been a set-up right from the beginning? What did he mean by all of this? Was this mere seduction? Or a gesture of kindness? Her heart thudded so fast she thought she might faint.

He strode forward from the throng of people and pulled her into a quick hug. 'I changed my mind about the party once we got to talking,' he whispered into her ear. 'I thought it would be more fun to have a party for you.'

Her fingers touched his smooth jacket briefly, the contact with his body *far* too brief. He pulled back and looked at her for a split second, a shot of truth in his gaze—serious, sweet sincerity.

So all the things he'd asked her about hadn't been for Lauren, but for her? No wonder he'd wanted to know which mousse *she'd* preferred. She blinked rapidly, emotion slamming into her. Pleasure, disbelief, gratitude, confusion.

She went cold again—and hot. She wanted this, she appreciated this, she did. But part of her wanted to escape as well. Part of her wanted to be alone.

Okay, not alone. She wanted to be with Brad.

* * *

Brad had lost all ability to move the moment he saw her. For a snatched moment of time his heart had stopped, his muscles froze solid, his brain shut down completely. When his system started again, it sped straight to a higher rate than usual. Adrenalin coursed through his veins and desire shot straight to his groin. Yeah, that was the part of him most affected. He drew a deep breath and forced his body to relax. Mya had made it more than clear it wasn't happening. And that was fine. He was man enough to handle rejection. Except she didn't look as if she was saying 'no' now. Her green eyes were wide and as fixed on him as his were on her. He'd known all along she was attracted to him, but determined not to have a hot affair. He could respect that. He was a man, not an animal, and all this tonight really hadn't been about trying to make it happen. Only now he finally saw it—the surrender in her eyes, the seduction.

The *yes*.

She was in that dress. That damn beautiful pink prom dress, with her breasts cupped high and ribbons trailing down her bare back. His attempt to hold back his body's reaction began to falter. When she looked at him like that? His muscles bunched, rigid with the urge to push her three steps back to the wall and screw her 'til she screamed. Nothing sophisticated, nothing smooth. Just a wild-animal moment to assuage the white-hot lust consuming him.

But they were in a roomful of people and that wasn't the show he had planned for them. And it wasn't what she truly wanted either. She had her other priorities and he could respect them, right?

The only way he'd get through the night alive was to stay away from her and focus on his host duties. He'd been crazy taking this on, on top of his overfull caseload. He'd challenge Mya for her 'world's most busy' title. But he'd done it. And that look on her face had been worth it. Now he could only hope she appreciated the other things he had planned for the evening. But jumping her wasn't on that list.

Mya was aware of Lauren watching her so she forced her gaze off Brad's tall frame as he disappeared back into the throng. 'This is unbelievable.' She smiled at her best friend.

'So good.' Lauren grabbed her hand. 'Come on, I heard a rumour about crazy cocktails.'

They were there—listed on a chalk-board with Jonny standing behind the bar rolling his eyes over the contents. Mya grinned and ordered the only alcohol-free option—she needed to keep her wits about her.

A crowd formed around her—friends she hadn't seen or been able to have fun with in ages, workmates with whom she'd never been able to just hang out. Conversation was fast and snatched and fun, and she tried so hard not to keep watch for Brad. She was determined to enjoy this—the first party ever thrown for her.

But an hour or so into it, the lights suddenly dimmed dramatically.

'What's happening?' Mya leaned close to Lauren as the music switched so suddenly nothing but fierce drumming hit max volume.

'I have no idea.'

Mya stared transfixed as about twenty black-clad figures swooped in, suddenly clearing a path through the crowds and pushing giant black boxes around the floor. The drums continued while the shadows put some kind of construction together.

Brad, looking sexier than a man had any right to be,

was suddenly lit up from an overhead spotlight and appeared taller than ever. She realised those black-clad figures had created a small stage of sorts that extended down the middle of the room. Mya, like everyone else in the place, was stunned into immobility.

'If you don't mind, everyone, there's something we need to do tonight.' Brad's voice boomed out. He had a microphone?

The black cloths that had been covering the windows behind him dropped, revealing two giant screens. The spotlight went off Brad while on screen an old-style countdown reel played. The guests joined in counting down. As they got to one the entire bar went pitch-black.

In the pregnant pause, Mya leaned in to Lauren. 'When did he set this up?'

'You're asking me?' Lauren giggled. 'He didn't let me in on this bit. I just had to get you here.'

'You know we're here to celebrate Mya's birthday tonight. But the thing that you and I all know, but that Mya doesn't quite believe yet, is that not only is she an amazing academic and gifted cocktail creator, she's also an artist. And so for tonight, we're turning this place into an art gallery and seeing what other marvellous things Mya has done.'

'He's *what*?' Mya asked, clapping her hand over her mouth to hold back the shriek.

Now she understood what the stage really was—a runway. And walking along the runway now were models. Slim, gorgeous girls in black bikinis and boots, modelling her hats, her accessories, her dresses that she'd created in her teen years and in the first couple of years at university. Where the hell had he got them all from?

She turned to Lauren, who held her hands up in

the classic 'don't shoot' pose and shook her head at the same time.

She glanced at Brad and couldn't contain the crow of delighted laughter. *Naturally* he'd found a way to get bikini-clad women on the scene. The crowd cheered and clapped, and she couldn't blame them as the leggy beauties strutted the length and Brad gave a running commentary on each item.

'There was a time in Mya's life when we all looked forward to seeing what it was she was wearing—the accessories, the clothes, sometimes the shoes.'

Everybody laughed as a picture of silver-marker-decorated gumboots flashed up on the screens.

'She moved into this world of recycled clothing, making new from the old, turning someone else's rubbish into art for herself. Maximalist, statement clothing. More than clothing. It was wearable art.'

Mya gazed at both stage and screen, her heart swelling. He'd created a multimedia display—a live modelling show interspersed with images from the past flashing up on those giant screens and a soundtrack made up of her fave teen beats. She pressed her freezing palm to her hot forehead. All those DJ picks he'd texted her. The really cheesy ones she'd sent back. He'd made a music mash-up and photo montage, and it was all so embarrassing and wonderful at the same time.

'Of course, she designed for men as well,' Brad said as the tempo of music changed.

Oh, my. Mya's jaw dropped and she gripped Lauren's hand, giggling now. Because she'd *never* designed anything for a guy. But there was an extremely buff guy up there now in nothing but black boxers and some sort of butchered baseball cap. She hadn't designed it for a man, though one could wear it, of course, but it had just been for the fun of it. And the tie that was now being displayed by another guy with very little else on, that had been her school tie that she'd redecorated in a rebellious fit one day. But that mega-buff guy in nothing but black boxers really knew how to show it off.

'So come on, everyone, give it up for Multifaceted Mya.'

Oh, no, someone had switched the lights on her. Literally shone the light on her, and some gorgeous thing came down to where she sat with Lauren. It was the buff guy with the cap. Nothing but the boxers and the cap. Mya looked over at Brad and saw his mouth twitching with amusement as he spoke.

'While Mya makes her way to the runway, here are a couple of stills from the collection where we can see her talent at her best.'

Mya froze on her seat. He couldn't be serious—she had to walk up there? And OMG there were huge photos of her up on those screens?

The black-clad male model extended his hand to her. She had no choice but to take her turn down the damn runway with the hot stuff at her side.

'Let's face it,' Brad concluded. 'The lady has an abundance of talent.'

Everyone in the place was on their feet and cheering.

Mya looked at Brad and saw his smile. Tender, a little mocking—self-mocking perhaps—but genuine. It pierced straight through the last thin layer of defence she had left and exposed her to the full glare of his attraction. In every cell, all the way to her toes it hit—how gorgeous he was.

He wasn't just sexy and funny and handsome. He was nice, thoughtful and caring. It was a side of him she'd never wanted to acknowledge. She'd preferred to keep him in the slutski spoilt-man stereotype. Mr Superficial Playboy. That was the easy way out. But the truth was he was utterly outrageous, utterly unashamed and yet utterly kind.

The lights came back on, and Lauren came up as the bar music resumed.

'It was all her idea.' Brad curved his arm around Lauren's shoulders and drew her close.

'That's not true.' Lauren shook her head firmly.

'Lauren found everything.' Brad gave his sister a sharp look.

'He came up with it when we were playing tennis at the club the other week.'

'It was supposed to be a party for you,' Mya said, too shaky inside to look at Brad at this moment.

'I don't need a party.' Lauren shrugged. 'I go to parties all the time.'

'I'm getting you back for your birthday,' Mya promised.

Lauren just laughed as one of her boys claimed her for the dance floor.

'How did you do all this?' Mya asked Brad, her mouth dry and still not looking at him.

'I had help,' he confessed. 'With the catwalk and the lighting and the music and stuff.'

Mya shook her head and looked across the room. 'Where did you find all of it?'

'My mother's itemised storage system. Lauren had kept them all.'

Well, it had mainly been Lauren's clothes Mya had messed with. The only thing Mya had kept was the dress she was now wearing.

'And you called on all your girlfriends to model for you.' She felt overwhelmed. 'Why did you do it?'

'I found some of the pictures of you,' he said softly.

'You and your pictures.' She stole a quick glance at him.

His mouth had twisted into a wry smile and that soft expression was in his eyes. 'None as good as the one you sent me, but ones Lauren took when you guys were mucking around a few years ago. You were so bold and so creative. Why have you given all that up? You have real talent.'

'No,' she scoffed, totally downplaying it.

'Didn't you just see that standing ovation?'

'You set it up.' She couldn't resist the urge to lean closer to tease him. 'All those beautiful models and all their glorious skin?'

Her words drew a reluctant smile to his lips. 'All that aside, you really do have talent,' he insisted.

'I appreciate this, so much,' she said softly, her throat aching because it was such a kind thing he'd done for her. 'But I don't have time to do that any more. It was a hobby. Life has moved on from that stuff.'

She blinked as bleak frustration dimmed his eyes. 'Mya, you don't *have* a life.'

'I do,' she argued, quiet but firm. 'And I'm lucky enough to have friends.' Ones who cared. She might even dare put him in that category after tonight. Except, grateful as she was for this night, she didn't want to lock him away in that neat and tidy box.

Something flashed in his eyes and was almost immediately blanked out. All that remained was resignation—she felt it too.

He smiled as another guest walked up to talk to them. It was that charismatic smile of his, yet strangely devoid of depth. Despite the excessive heat of a crowded clubfloor on a hot summer's night, Mya's skin cooled as if

the first spears of winter had bitten their way through
the hot warehouse bricks. His walls were back up; that
automatic charming gleam hid the honesty in his eyes.
It felt as if she'd lost something precious.

Brad watched her mingle, the gnawing feeling inside
worsening with each minute that she laughed and in-
teracted and clearly had fun. She was having a great
time, but it wasn't enough. He was used to getting what
he wanted—easily. Giving up what he wanted wasn't
nearly so easy. Especially when she looked at him with
that expression in her eyes—the one that told him he
could have what he'd wanted more than anything these
past couple of weeks.

But successful though it may be to a point, this night
was also a failure. She'd appreciated his effort, but she
hadn't understood it. He wanted her to understand she
had so much more to offer the world if she'd just give
herself a chance, if she just let go of all the burden she
took on and let herself be free. She should be doing
the things she loved, not just doing things *for* those she
loved.

The realisation hurt and with that came the worse
hit—he cared too much about where she was at and
what she was doing. When he looked at her now, there
wasn't just that stirring in his groin—there was an ache
in his chest.

He liked her—too much to mess around with her.
Things don't end all that well for your women. While
he wasn't sure he agreed with Lauren's statement, he
wasn't taking the risk with Mya. He could get her to say
yes, but she wasn't cut out for a fling, and he didn't want
more than just that. Even if he did, she wasn't ready for

that in her life. She had her other priorities and that was fine. The only thing to do, right now, was walk away.

So he did.

CHAPTER EIGHT

IT MIGHT have been one of the best nights of her life, but Mya wanted the fireworks to finish it off. She didn't want to be the wallflower walking home alone tonight as she had all those years ago at that miserable prom.

She glanced around. Lauren was flirting with yet another guy—she'd been collecting them throughout the night. Several other friends were propping up the bar getting outrageously hammered with her lethal cocktail mix. Others were up on the catwalk having a dance-off to the hits of their teen years. It was a crazy-fun night.

But Brad had quietly slipped off into the dark—alone. He hadn't said goodbye to her or anyone. He'd flipped a wave at Lauren but he hadn't even looked at Mya.

That wasn't good enough.

Did he think he could do this for her—send her insides into such a spin—and then walk away?

Tonight had been her one night off in months. And didn't she deserve pleasure in it—pleasure for *all* the night? Didn't she deserve a treat? It wouldn't be like that mess-up last year when she'd thought she could handle a night of nothing but physical fun and had failed. This time she knew what she was doing—and she *knew* Brad. She even liked him. But not enough to cause confusion. She'd read the rulebook, was certain she could handle herself on the field. This time she already knew the score. And while there was that hint of insecurity about her performance, she figured Brad wouldn't be all that bothered. Ultimately all she'd be was another notch to him, right? But *she* would have the best sexual experience of her life. He'd teased that it would be, but she knew to her bones he'd follow through. She simply couldn't resist—not for one night.

So she blew Lauren a kiss and waved.

Her feet moved of their own accord, fast, determined, sure. She was stone-cold sober but in a blink she was there already—standing at his front door. Before she could take a breath and think better of it, she hammered the door so hard her knuckles hurt.

He opened it sooner than she expected. He'd lost the jacket but was still in the black shirt and trousers and, oddly, a cleaning cloth in his hand. He stared at her— saying it all with just that wild-eyed look—surprise to desire in a heartbeat. Only then he closed his eyes and bent his head. Sudden nerves paralysed her. Insecurity drowned her moment of boldness.

'Are you going to let me in?' she asked, her voice pathetically breathy even to her own ears. So much for chutzpah.

He looked up and she saw nothing but raw emotion in his eyes—not just desire, but torment. It was reflected in his stance too as he blocked her entry, his hand gripping the door. 'You know what will happen if I do.'

Relief shot into her belly, bursting into flame on impact. 'Yes,' she said. 'That's why I'm here.'

'But—'

'I don't want a relationship, and I don't want a fling. But I've changed my mind about the one-night thing.'

He swallowed and then stepped to one side. She

walked in, holding her head high while her blood fizzed round her body. She went straight to the place she'd fantasised about for weeks. The cover was stripped back, the light switched on—the brightness harsh on her eyes after the moonlit walk here.

'What happened to the vase?' The mess on the floor surprised her.

'Accident caused by frustration.' He watched her as if he was afraid she'd disappear if he blinked.

'You're not usually clumsy.'

'I'm not usually frustrated.'

She paused. If he was 'frustrated', why wasn't he happy to see her here now? 'Why are you feeling bad?' she asked softly, stepping closer. 'It was a great night. I loved every second of it. Everyone else did too.'

'This isn't why I did it.' He spoke low and rough. 'I just wanted you to have some fun.'

'I did,' she answered. 'And I'd like some more.'

'Lauren said not to mess with you. That you're fragile.'

Shock hit, embarrassment soon followed and both burned. What else had Lauren said? 'Do I look fragile to you?'

'Not on the outside, but that vase didn't seem that fragile either and it still broke when I dropped it.'

'You're not going to get the opportunity to drop me,' she said. 'I only want what's left of tonight. I don't want anything more. I'd never expect promises from you. I understand that.' There were only a couple of hours of darkness left. A couple would have to be enough. 'And you know I can't give more either. This isn't going to be anything more for either of us. This is just tonight.'

He walked nearer. Intensity sliced into her as she saw the look on his face, the raw, unrestrained desire honed in on one focal point—*her*. Excitement swept over her and she backed up until the backs of her thighs hit his bed and she sat on the edge of it.

She gazed at him—unashamed in her admiration. He was so much taller, stronger. And looking at her like this? So lethal.

She realised that until now he'd kept a leash on his desires, letting her think she'd controlled this thing between them. But he could have pulled her to him any time he'd wanted. His potency was strong enough to render her will useless. She wanted to be his. But just as violent was the desire to have him ache for her in this same extreme way. Impossible, of course. Hence the one night.

'Are you sure?' he asked as he moved to within touching distance.

'Yes.'

'I like you.' He frowned as if that wasn't a good thing. 'I want the best for you.'

She just wanted to enjoy this attraction—and end up free of it. 'Then give me the best.'

He smiled, his eyes lighting up.

'Don't tease me any more,' she begged. She needed him to come nearer, to stop talking, to make her feel as if she wasn't about to make a massive fool of herself.

'But it's all about the tease.' A glimpse of humour.

'You know what I mean.' She wanted it to be fast. She wanted to get the release, to be freed from it. For it to be over.

He stepped close. The brilliant thing about the height of his bed was that she didn't have to crane her neck too far to look at him. With a single finger he traced the hem of her dress—now rucked up to just over her knees. She couldn't believe he wasn't moving faster already. But instead he put his hands on her pressed-together knees and exerted the smallest pressure.

'Let me in, Mya.' His gaze didn't leave her face. 'Let me in.'

Mya trembled at the cool command. He seemed to be asking for more than access to her body. 'I am.' She swung her legs wide.

'No.' He bent and his lips brushed her neck. 'If we're doing this, then I want everything tonight.' He ran two fingers down her cheek; the slight pressure made her turn her head. He whispered into her exposed ear. His words a caress, an intimacy. As if he'd somehow accessed her soul. 'How much do you want this?' His lips brushed the whorls of her ear. 'It better be as much as I do because otherwise you might not be able to keep up.'

'You're that fabulous, huh?'

'I just want to be sure we're on the same page for this evening. Because it ain't over.'

'I'm not fat and I'm not about to sing,' she said with a hint of her old defiance.

'What about screaming?' He leaned closer until there was nothing but a whisper of air between them. She could feel the heat radiating from him, and her own emotions burned.

Tired of talk, tired of waiting, Mya wanted action.

She lifted her chin and laid one on him.

For a moment Brad lost control of the situation. For someone who supposedly suffered extreme sensitivity, Mya could give a blisteringly hard kiss. Her fingers threaded into his hair, holding him there while beneath his mouth hers was lush and hungry. Startled, he gave it to her—the full brunt of the want that had burdened him these past weeks. He dived deep into her sweet

mouth, tangling his tongue against her equally raven-
ous one. He pressed harder until he felt her trembling
and moaning already.

He eased it back a bit, put his hands on her face, cupping those beautiful cheekbones with gentle fingers and
pulling back just enough for their lips to barely be clinging. 'I have no intention of bruising you,' he said quietly.

That nagging feeling that she was holding back
wouldn't leave him. What held her so reserved? While
she smiled and joked with the bar patrons and Lauren's
boys, there was that distance that he'd seen no one
breach. He wanted to be the one who broke all the way
in.

So while there was a time and a place for hot and
hard, quick and rough sex, this wasn't it. She wanted it
that way. He knew she did. She was desperate to have
him to have the release. And for it to be over. Because
there was that part of her that was mad with herself for
wanting him as badly as she did. She didn't want to be
another of his conquests. She didn't understand yet that
she *wasn't*.

Because there was his own confounding desire for
her to come to terms with. He hadn't realised it was possible to want a woman this much. He'd craved sex before. Of course he had. But that had been sex. That had
been about getting the pleasure and the release. This was
about her. This was about seeing her shaking and out of
control and filled with ecstasy. This was about seeing
her weak with wanting him, with her unable to stand—
only being able to lie on a bed and beg for him to come
to her. Oh, yeah, the submissive fantasies were a first.

And now he had her—lying back on his bed with
that dress even more rucked up, giving him a glimpse of
lace-covered treasure. He tensed every muscle to fight

the urge to dive straight in. Heat tightened his skin; he felt as if he were on the rack—stretched well beyond his usual limitations. And now she forced him closer than he'd like. Pushed him to intrude deeper than he normally would. Yes, he wanted it all from her.

He quickly stripped himself and then straddled her on the bed and let the ribbons slide through his fingers as he loosened them enough to pull the bodice of the dress down to bare her beautiful, bountiful breasts.

She shivered before he even touched them. He let his fingers trace near to their precious peaks, so slowly and gently—watching to see how she coped. She moved restlessly beneath him. He bent closer, traced his tongue around the tight, rosy nipples and blew warm air over the tips of them.

She shuddered.

'Too much?' he asked softly.

She shook her head, her chest rising and falling quickly. He carefully cupped her soft flesh, let the centre of his palm touch her nipple. She shuddered again and arched her back, pushing her breasts deeper into his hands. He pushed his hands together, pushing her breasts together, letting her nipples peep over the top of his cupped hands. Beautiful. Big and beautiful and so responsive. He blew on them again. And then so carefully bent to brush his lips over them.

'Oh, no,' she whimpered.

'Okay?' he murmured, caressing them ever so softly.

She nodded and arched towards him again so he kept up the slow, wet caresses.

Her hips rocked now and he smiled at her giveaway reaction. Did she want the same treatment down there? He sure as hell hoped so. He stripped away her small briefs and then kissed his way down her flat stomach, his own excitement uncontrollable as he neared her most intimate curves. He'd dreamed of this for so long, he could hardly believe it was real now. But she was warm and writhing and tasted so hot. Her response deepened, her movements wild.

The pleasure of seeing her so wanting was more satisfying than anything in his life. He peeled her legs further apart, tasting her glistening femininity, holding her hips firmly so she couldn't escape him as she stiffened and then began to convulse. He sucked on her most sensitive nub and then buried his tongue inside her, quickly reaching up to cup her breasts and cover her nipples—diamond hard now, they pressed into his palms. He applied more pressure and tasted the reward as she came hard and loud, screaming for him.

He breathed hard, flicking his tongue to see her through the aftershocks and then he moved quickly. But his fingers were all thumbs as he tried to get the condom on.

'Damn,' he muttered. Desperate, the need to drive deep within her the only thing circling in his head.

Now. Now. Now.

His lungs burned, his heart thumped—and he'd not even started. He was going to embarrass himself at this rate.

'Can I help?' she teased.

'No,' he snapped hoarsely. Instantly feeling bad about biting her head off.

But she laughed. A throaty, sexy laugh as if she knew just how he was feeling.

It was all right for her—she'd had her first orgasm. Finally he was sheathed. He knelt and gazed at her. His gaze fixed on the cherry-red, too-sensitive nipples, lowered to her pink, glistening sex and then he looked up into her glowing eyes.

His heart seized.

Her laughter faded. 'Brad?'

Her voice lifted a notch, the return of excitement even though she perceived the threat. Oh, yeah, he had plans. He leaned over her, relishing using his size to dominate her. But she wasn't intimidated. Not her, no—her smile returned. Those wide, uneven lips parted and revealed that sexy-as-hell gap. All petite, fragile, strong woman.

Take. Take. Take.

So he did. Peeling her legs further apart, he took position, his aching erection pressing against her slippery, sweet entrance. So hot for him. Meeting his gaze unflinchingly, her breasts rising and falling fast as she waited for him to finally take her.

And he did—surging forward to encase himself in one swift movement. But he was almost obliterated as he felt her clamp around him for the first time. He closed his eyes, clenched his teeth, locked still to stop the instant orgasm before he'd begun any kind of rhythm. That just *wasn't* happening.

He breathed hard, pushing back the blissful, delirious fog, refusing his release until he'd seen her too strung out to scream any more. And finally he moved, slow, back and forth, circular. Stopping to caress her breasts, her neck, her lips. Teasing, nipping, sucking—savouring every inch of skin he could access while locking himself inside her. And it was good. So damn good.

'Please let me come, please let me come,' she begged him, writhing again, her face flushed and her skin damp.

Victory sang in his veins as he slowly claimed, withdrew and reclaimed his place right in the core of her. Her clenching, soft heat offered unutterable joy as much as it did wicked torment. And he was too ecstatic to care about the implications of the one thought hammering in his head.

Mine. Mine. Mine.

Breathless, pinned beneath his marvellous weight, Mya called to him. How could he bear it so slow? Wasn't he dying inside for the release? How could he hold back from coming inside her so long? Didn't he want to drive himself into her the way she ached for him to—furious and fast and hard?

Oh, hell—was it her? Was she not good enough at this for him? She certainly didn't know any tricks or anything much beyond the basics. And this was sex at its most basic, with him above her, no fancy positions or toys. She knew no tricks—was probably the most apathetic lover he'd ever had. All she'd been able to do the past half-hour was lie there and moan.

He slipped his palm beneath her bottom, pushing her closer so he could thrust even deeper into her, and all self-conscious thought was obliterated in the ecstasy of his onslaught. There was nothing she could do but absorb his decadent attention.

She tensed as that unbearably tense pleasure rebuilt in her. He pushed closer, closer. Her body tautened, her muscles, nerves, heart all strung out, locking onto every part of him she could. She was no longer begging, no longer coherent. Just gasping, grasping for that final step into oblivion. And then screaming. He tossed her into that river of delight. Sensations tumbled over and over—bliss shuddering through her in spasm after spasm. And she clung to him through it all as if he were her life raft as well as the source of the surge.

She gasped again as the last tremor shivered through her and she regained enough strength to sweep a hand down his sweat-slicked back. His skin burned, the muscles beneath flexing and rigid. She turned her face into his neck, wanting to hide how raw her emotions were. How close she felt to him in this moment.

With a feral grunt he pulled her head back so her mouth met his. A hungry, uncontrollable kiss. His tongue pummelling as fast and relentlessly as that other part of him was. Something broke free within her, that desire to *hold* onto him. To hold onto him so tight because he'd given her something so precious. She sucked on his tongue the way her sex was—tightly squeezing. Not letting him go. Stroking him back. A slick friction that set fire to her senses again.

He tore his mouth from hers, arching and shouting as his release ripped out of him. Her body quaked as she received it, intensifying her own pleasure to the point where she could bear no more.

It took a few moments for Brad to realise he'd blanked out and was slumped over her. Their bodies were stuck together—hot skin, locked limbs. Hell, could she breathe? He propped himself up on his elbows and looked at her.

'Wow.' She nodded slowly. 'Okay. I can see why.'

It wasn't quite the comment he'd wanted. That hadn't been his usual wham and bam and 'let's do it three times again, ma'am'. Physical and fast and fun. He didn't know what had got into him with this so-slow-you-think-you're-going-to-die-from-bliss intensity.

'You sure proved your point.' She swallowed.

He might have managed to laugh that off if he weren't so winded. Slowly, reluctantly, painfully, he withdrew from her warmth and rolled to lie beside her. He kept his eyes closed, holding back the exposed feeling. Because that had been so far from his usual behaviour that he couldn't comprehend it.

That hadn't just been sex. He didn't really know what it had been, but he knew it was not just sex. Part of him wanted to flee the scene immediately. Another part of him was stirring back to life, hungry for a repeat. How could the gnawing ache be worse now than it had been before?

'I'm sorry for being so useless,' she murmured.

He flashed his eyes open and lifted his head. *'What?'*

To his amazement she'd gone bright red, more flushed than when she'd been in the throes of passion and about to come. 'I just lay there.'

He really did laugh then—and it was all genuine. 'No, you didn't.'

She'd sighed and moved in subtle, uncontrollable ways that had nearly driven him out of his mind. And she'd held him. He'd had the most incredible feeling when she'd held him.

He pulled her close. But sleep didn't claim him as quickly as it did her. Instead he lay still fully attuned to the signals of her body, his embrace tightening as her body relaxed into sleep. He'd never struggled to get to sleep after sex before. But he'd never had sex like that before either. He tried to process it, his body humming, his mind replaying fragments, sending flashes of memory to senses already overloaded and struggling with oversensitivity. Almost an hour later, still nowhere near sleep, he slipped away from her. In the moonlit kitchen he poured a glass of water. He drank, trying to wash away the fever and regain his laid-back, carefree attitude. But the cool water didn't dispel the growing sense of discomfort and confusion.

The best moment of his life might also have been the biggest mistake.

CHAPTER NINE

MYA woke early, panic clanging louder than an electronic alarm plugged into subwoofer speakers. Warm, sweat-dampened skin where they touched. Time to get out of here. She slipped out from his hot embrace, ultra-careful not to wake him because there was something she had to do first.

Quietly she found her phone and got it ready. Just as he stirred, she threw the sheet back and captured him in all his morning glory before he could blink.

'Now we're even.' She laughed and teasingly waved the phone at him, determined to hide the ache pulling down her heart—from herself most of all.

He blinked and a slow, naughty smile spread over his face—the return of the charmer. 'Damn, you should have told me.' He stretched. 'I could have posed better for you.'

He could *never* have been posed better. He looked like the Greek god he'd joked about.

'I'll delete this when you delete the picture of me,' she offered. But it was a lie. Even if she trashed it from her phone, she couldn't ever wipe this image from her brain.

'I'm never deleting that.' His laughter rumbled, rippling muscles over his taut, bronzed chest. 'I've sent it to my computer. It looks brilliant on a big screen.'

Oh, she should have known. 'You're a perv.'

'And you're an amateur. You think I mind you having a photo of me like this?'

'Well.' Mya sniffed. 'I guess half the city's women have seen you like this, so, really, it's nothing that personal, is it?' She had to remind herself who she was dealing with—and all that this had been.

'Miaow,' he said and then reared up on the bed, moving towards her like a tiger on the prowl. 'Why don't we make a movie instead? Come here and star in it with me.'

The sight of him on all fours was almost enough to tip her over the edge, but she dug in her heels. 'You really are a perv.'

'Come on, back to bed.' He knelt right up, the most X-rated fantasy Mya had ever seen. 'It's early.'

'And I have work to get to.' She really *had* to get out of here.

'You're kidding.'

She shook her head.

'Be late. Call in sick.'

Oh, no, she wasn't letting him tempt her. It was finished. 'You know it's over. The mystery is gone—the wondering of "what'll we be like"—now we know. Now you can go back to your three-women-a-week lifestyle and I can get on with my studying.'

There was a moment, the briefest of pauses when she wondered what he was going to say. He looked away, hiding his expressive eyes, and he flung back on the bed. 'It's only three when I'm on holiday.' He rested his head on his arm and looked even more like a Greek god reclining.

And all Mya could think was how he'd said there was nothing like starting the day with some good sex. She closed her eyes and forced away the whisper of temptation and the vision of one very aroused Brad. She had a shift to get to. She pulled her crumpled dress back on, hoping it was early enough for her not to get caught doing the walk of shame home.

'You can borrow some of my clothes if you want,' he said unhelpfully.

No. That would mean she'd have to see him again to return them, and there was no way that was happening. There was no way she was indulging again. It was going to take long enough to forget how incredible he was as a lover.

She didn't regret last night. But it had been so good she almost did.

'I don't think they'd fit but thanks all the same.' She turned her back on him so he couldn't see her mega blush.

There was no reason for them to see each other again after this. He'd had what he'd wanted now and so had she. It was over. Outside work hours she'd be back to nothing but study, and he'd be back to saving kids during the day and romping his way around the city at night. It was one night and it was over.

Four days later her eyes hurt and she was exhausted but two coffees and a sugary doughnut saw her through the first two hours of her shift at the café. She'd already agreed to stay on and do a double shift before going straight to the bar. Desperate to fill every moment of her day. Study wasn't enough—it was in silence, and in silence her mind wandered. She needed noise and relentless activity.

Sex was sex, right? It was fun and physical, the release was great, and then it was over. Nothing more to it. So why was she so damn fixated on him?

Drew looked up when she finally got to the bar. She was running late from the café, but to her surprise he wasn't grumpy; in fact he smiled at her as if she were his employee of the week.

'We have another private function tonight,' he said. 'In the VIP room.'

'We do?' Another person had hired out part of the place for some outrageous price this close to Christmas? 'Who's the client?'

'Same guy as last time,' Drew answered. 'Brad. He specially requested Jonny. Double rates.'

Mya's insides went solar-hot and her outsides ice-cold, while her heart soared and then dropped in the space of a second. He was supposed to be out of her life—in fact, he *was* out of her life. He hadn't contacted her; she hadn't contacted him... But now he was coming to her place of work but didn't want to see her? He'd asked for *Jonny*?

She didn't know whether to be mad, glad or amused.

'Trouble is,' Drew said, 'Jonny cut himself today. His fingers are all bandaged up and he'll be off the rest of the week. Are you up to serving the private party?'

'Do I still get double rates?' Mya asked.

'I'll have to check with the client.'

Mya flicked her fringe out of her eyes and got down to prepping her cocktail trims. 'Don't worry, I'll check with him.' Her blood quickened as both anger and anticipation simmered. Why hadn't he wanted *her* to tend his bar, hmm?

Half an hour later, she walked into the small room that could be roped off for VIPs or small private functions. 'Hi, Brad,' she said coolly. 'You've offended me.'

'I have?'

'You don't like my cocktail skills any more?'

'I didn't think you'd want me to pay for your time.'

He turned on the smiling charm immediately—but then leaned a little closer to where she now stood setting up the small bar. 'I thought you might prefer not to have to see me.'

She shrugged. 'It wouldn't matter to me.' She carefully placed glasses. 'Maybe I could do with the money.'

'And that wouldn't bother you?' He watched her closely.

'You'd be paying me to pour drinks,' she answered with some sass. 'Not anything else. And you're offering to pay Jonny more than the going rate?'

'To secure the private space I had to. I didn't think you'd want me to treat you as a charity.'

'But you wouldn't be, would you?' she asked coolly.

He studied her, a small smile playing around his way-too-luscious lips. Yeah, there was the problem—she now knew exactly how skilled that mouth was.

'I can be professional,' she said—to herself more than to him.

'Can you?'

'Sure, can't you?'

His smile deepened. 'I'm not at work. I'm here to have fun and flirt with the bar staff.'

'You wanted to flirt with Jonny?' She laughed. 'I'm sorry to disappoint you, but Jonny is off sick. You're stuck with me.'

He looked at her.

'Am I worth double?' she asked him and tilted her head on the side.

'You do know what you're doing, don't you?'

'Stirring a cocktail, yes?'

'You're stirring, but not just the cocktail.'

'We can still be friends, right? Isn't that what you said?' she said archly.

That was before they'd slept together.

'Of course.' He inclined his head and walked to greet the first person coming through the door.

Mya watched the guests arrive and insecurity smote her—there were women here, seriously hot women. Smart ones too. Lawyers, the lot of them. And it was so dumb to feel threatened when she was ninety per cent on her way to being a lawyer too. And even if she weren't, she still didn't need to feel any less worthy than them.

Yet she did. The years of conditioning at that school had shaped her—that she should feel grateful for having that opportunity. That she shouldn't stuff it up. That her drop-kick family background meant she'd never be fully accepted by the social strata that most of these people came from—as James had pointed out.

She watched Brad laughing with one of the women. Oh, no, maybe that was why he hadn't wanted her to work the bar—had he been sparing her because he was here with another woman? Why hadn't she thought of that?

Brad knew all the guys were checking her out. It had been a dumb idea to come here, but he'd thought he could pull it off if Jonny had been doing the work. Then Brad could pop into the main bar and snatch a few words with Mya and see how the land lay. Only now she was right in front of him, smiling, joking and teasing with them all as she served them.

And all he could do was watch like some lovelorn pup hoping for any kind of bone to be thrown his way. Some small scrap that might show she wanted him again. It was more than his pride that was stung. Did she really not want another night with him? Had that truly been enough for her? He didn't believe it—was egotistical enough not to. All he needed was some proof. And to get that, he figured he just needed to get a little closer to her.

Mya fully regretted saying she'd do this. He was more handsome than she remembered, more fun with his wicked smiles and sharp words. And now she was assailed by images of sneaking him into the cupboard or some dark corner in the alley and having her wicked way with him. Quick and frantic and fabulous.

And to make it worse, he'd now taken up residence right beside her and was watching her every move with the full-on maple-syrup glow. Brad Davenport on full throttle. She fumbled with the bottle and was annoyed to glance up and see him suddenly smiling as if he'd won the lottery.

'Not on your game tonight?' he drawled. 'Or is it because you can't concentrate when I'm near?'

She stopped what she was doing—but couldn't stop her blush. 'Don't be mean.'

His brows hit the ceiling. 'I'm not the one who was mean—you're the one who said one night only,' he whispered harshly as he leaned over.

'You only *do* one night,' she whispered back.

'Not necessarily.' He leaned against the bar. 'Maybe I can do unpredictable.'

Mya clutched the neck of the bottle with damp fingers and tried to joke. 'Would you be saying this to Jonny?'

He didn't bother to reply, just kept those burning brown eyes on her.

'Why didn't you ask for me?' she added.

'Can you honestly say you wouldn't have got mad if I did? Can you honestly say you'd be happy for me to pay for your time no matter the context?'

She poured herself a tall glass of water. Damn, the guy actually understood her.

'I'll walk you home tonight,' he said.

'You're hoping for a good-night kiss?' She squared her shoulders and asked straight out.

'I'm concerned for your safety,' he replied, his eyes twinkling.

'Really?'

'Partly. Mainly I want more than a good-night kiss.'

'Do you?' she asked softly. 'What do you want?'

He didn't answer with words—just that look.

Mya turned away while she still could. 'I'll get Pete to come in and finish serving you guys, and I'll meet you out the front at closing time.'

To her pleasure, he was waiting as she'd asked, at the very end of the night.

'Where do you live?' he asked.

'Tonight?' she said. 'I'm staying at your place.' She walked up to him but he took a step to the side and back, out of reach.

'I'm not touching you now,' he muttered. 'If I touch you now we'll be all over each other in the nearest shadow and I don't want to do that.'

'You don't?' Her confidence surged at his words.

He closed his eyes. 'I don't want it to be sordid.'

Delight and desire filled her, topped off with relief. All that pleasure was smashed away by the need that pierced her a second later. She walked faster. 'It wouldn't be.'

He stopped on the footpath behind her. 'Mya.' A warning, a plea, a demand.

She turned her head to look back at him and smiled.

Then she walked faster still, her body slick and ready. 'It would be fun.'

As it had been the night of her party, she seemed to fly rather than walk. Her feet skimmed over the concrete. There was no alcohol in her system, yet she was in a haze as if she was under the influence.

She was under the influence of *him*.

She realised he was breathing faster than normal, and he was fit. The walk home hadn't exactly taxed him. Something else was bothering him—the same thing that was bothering her.

She walked up the narrow path to his villa. Under the veranda they were shrouded in darkness the streetlamps couldn't penetrate. The scent of the rose in the pot by the door was sweet and fresh. She stood in front of the door, like an impatient cat yowling to be let in, while he stood behind her.

'I can't get the key in the lock,' he muttered, nuzzling her neck. 'Don't go getting all Freudian on that.' He chuckled with a groan.

At least they were almost inside his home. He hauled her closer, crushing her against him. She melted into his hot strength, almost delirious with ecstasy already. Yes, this was what she wanted—more of him. *All* of him. And she was too desperate now to wait a minute longer. On the darkened deck, no one could see them from the street. So Mya, bolder than she'd ever been in her life and on the brink of ecstasy because he wanted her as much as she did him, pulled her jeans down. She didn't get them very far, wiggling her hips side to side to tug them as far as she could, but she only made it to mid-thigh. She'd hooked her knickers with them, and despite the warmth of summer, the air on her bared butt was cool. She pressed back to feel the rough denim of his jeans against her.

He swore, pithy, crude, hot.

She looked over her shoulder as she put her hands to the cool paint and arched back, letting her butt grind against his pelvis.

He swore again, explicit and thrilling, and curled a strong arm around her waist, his other hand scraping the key in the lock. Finally he got it and turned the handle. He lifted her with that one arm and took the two paces inside. He turned them both and slammed the door, stepped forward immediately, his hands gripping hers and lifting them higher on the wood so they were above her head.

His feet moved between hers, pushing hers wider apart. But they couldn't go that far the way her jeans were only pulled to her mid-thigh. It excited her all the more—she wanted to be pinned by him again. It had been all she'd been able to think of for days. He leaned against her from behind, holding her still as he unzipped his jeans. She pressed her palms to the door herself, rubbing to feel the blunt head of him so near to entering her slick heat.

'Hell, Mya.' He cursed again. 'I want you...'

She heard the sharp rip, felt his movement behind her. A second later his hands circled her thighs. His fingers met in the middle, touching her intimately. She heard his roughly drawn breath as he felt how wet she already was. His fingers returned to her inner thighs, holding her tight now, and he thrust in hard. No preliminaries, just raw heat.

She gasped, shocked and delighted and desperate all at once. She put her hands on the door, bracing and giving leverage to push back on him and take him deeper.

He moaned and immediately pressed his mouth to her shoulder to muffle the sounds of ecstatic agony.

Heat beaded all over her body. Her breath burned in too-short bursts. More moisture slicked where she needed it most, easing his sudden, forceful invasion.

He circled his hips and then thrust hard all the way home again, surging into a quick, hard, breathless rhythm. A coarse word of bliss rapidly transformed into a groan and he paused his rough thrusts into her. 'Damn it…you can't possibly come this way.'

'Oh, yeah?' But she could, she was almost there already. Desperately turned on. 'Don't you dare stop.'

He lifted her, flattening her against the door. Literally screwing her to it. A good thing given her legs were trembling so much they couldn't hold her up because she was so close to orgasm.

He forced his fingers between her and the wood, and for a second they stroked, as if to ensure she was as turned on as she declared. She pressed against his hand, trapping it, stopping the tease. Then arched her back as much as she could.

'Brad!'

He growled and withdrew his hand, slamming it against the wall by her head as he thrust hard again. 'I want you so much.'

She squeezed her eyes shut, breathing hard as his words struck like hot stones into her soul and his body rammed once more into hers. She felt his rough jaw against her cheek; the blunt demand inflamed her body.

She could hardly move her mouth to form the words. 'More,' she confessed. 'I…want you. More… More.'

It became a mantra and then a scream as the sensations skidded, becoming convulsions that twisted through her. Her hands curled into claws as she shook.

She ground her hips round and round between him and the wall. Both immovable forces. With a harsh groan he resisted her attempts to milk him. His hands gripped her hips, holding her still as over and over he stroked as if trying to get deeper and deeper within her, as if he too couldn't bear for it to be over just yet. His need shocked her. The same need that had summoned her here, making her ignore both caution and reason.

'Oh. *Yes*.' Her own primal reaction to his demand was an orgasm so strong she would have fallen to the floor had he not held her so tightly.

His fingers dug as the answering cry was ripped from him.

Breathing hard, he slumped against her, still pinning her to the wall, his head falling to her shoulder. She felt the harsh gusts of breath down her back as he held her close. She appreciated the contact—the comfort—as if he too needed the time and the proximity to process what they'd just shared.

And then he moved, lifting her into his arms and stomping a few feet into his spare room—the library. He sank into the big armchair, holding her in his lap.

Their eyes met in the dim light. He smiled at her and then kissed her. She kissed him back. The slow, tender kisses that they'd skipped in their haste for completion.

'We're doing this again,' he said quietly.

How could she deny him anything when he was so skilfully stirring her body into blissful submission? 'A couple more times,' she muttered, barely able to think.

'More than a couple.'

Okay, she could see the attraction in that for her, but what about him? 'What's in it for you?'

He laughed silently, but she felt the vibrations all around her. 'You have to ask, after *that*?'

She'd never thought of herself as a skilled lover or any kind of sexual goddess. 'That other guy told me I was lousy in bed,' she admitted. 'And given James had just dumped me, I thought he was right.'

'You're kidding,' Brad groaned. 'You're amazing. That was unbelievably amazing.'

The glow he'd already lit inside her burned brighter. 'Is this not normal for you?' she teased.

He stilled. She could sense him deliberating over his reply. She looked away, studying the shelf of books as if she could read the titles in the gloom.

He took her chin in firm fingers and turned her so she had to look him in the eye again. 'No. It's not.'

She felt her cheeks burn but he wouldn't let her turn her head away.

'That other night? And tonight?' he said softly. 'Best sex of my life.'

'No,' she whispered. She didn't want him to flatter her with false praise.

'Do I have to print out a certificate before you'll believe me?'

She chuckled.

He was the one shaking his head now. 'You don't have to get the awards, you know. You don't need accolades to be certified attractive. All you have to do is smile.'

How could she not smile when he said things like that? 'Another confession?' she whispered. 'It was the best sex of my life too.'

He smiled.

'But this can't be anything,' she added quickly.

'I don't think we need to label it, do we?'

'It's only for a little while.' Only until she had her desire for him under control. If she didn't put her heart on the line, she'd be fine.

He shook his head. 'Don't you get it? We can't put limitations on this because we'll both want more if we do that. You always want what you can't have. And we both have that fighter within who wants to defy the rules.'

'So what do you suggest—no rules?'

'No rules.' He leaned over her and whispered. His hand teasing the soft skin of her inner thigh. 'And if you like, no boundaries.'

Mya stared at him, incredibly tempted. He meant physical boundaries. She knew that. 'None at all?'

He lifted his shoulders.

Her heart thudded so hard. 'All or nothing?'

'Anything you want me to do, sure, I'll do.'

'You're offering to be my love slave? You'll do whatever I want?' She couldn't help but smile at that idea.

He nodded. 'You take pleasure from me and I'll take pleasure from you.'

He was offering a licence to thrill. 'What if I don't want to do something you ask me to?' she asked curiously.

His expression deepened and he ran a gentle finger down her arm. 'I think you'll want to.'

She touched her tongue to her lip. Yes, she figured she would.

His fingers tickled as he suddenly grinned. 'I wasn't actually thinking of anything that kinky,' he teased. 'But maybe you were.'

Colour heated her cheeks. 'What I think of as kinky you probably think of as tame,' she muttered defensively.

'You can ask me for anything,' he murmured.

She nodded. 'It's not the right time for a relationship for me and you never want one...but for now—'

'There's just now.' His arms tightened around her and he stood, carrying her down to his room.

Mya reached out and switched on the light as they passed it.

'I love this wallpaper.' She gazed at the green vines climbing the white paper. 'It still stuns me you're into floral.'

'It's not floral,' he said firmly, planting her on the bed and tugging off her jeans. 'It's jungle.'

'*That's* floral.' She rolled onto her stomach and pointed to the small vase on the bedside table filled with sweet-smelling summer roses.

'Women like flowers,' he said blandly, bending to kiss the small of her back.

Oh, he might talk all sophisticated loverman, but it wasn't quite as it seemed and she knew it. 'No, you had flowers there that first time I visited, and you didn't know I was coming.'

'I'm always prepared for an overnight female guest.' He emphasised the tease with a nip of his teeth.

'No.' She rolled to face him and grabbed a fistful of his shirt to pull him onto her. 'You prefer to sleep at their houses so you can do the "quickie and exit" in the morning. The only reason *I'm* here is because you know I'll leave early. You know I'm not going to linger and make for an awkward morning-after moment.' She met his darkened gaze and determinedly ignored the way his fingers were stroking closer and closer to her nipple. 'So the flowers are here because you like them. Furthermore—'

'There's more?'

'Oh, there is. I have all the evidence for this case. You grow the roses in your garden.'

'Okay, so I grow the roses,' he admitted. 'Are you going to tease me about it?'

'Of course not.' She rubbed her fingers against his stubble. 'They're beautiful.'

His amusement turned wicked. 'I get pleasure from watching something bloom. I appreciate form, nature's "curves".' His hand slid over her hips and between her thighs.

'You can try to hide behind some sexy talk, but the fact is *you're* talented. You really care about your roses.'

'I really like curves.' He burrowed down the bed more. 'I like pretty pink flowers too.' He pulled her knees apart. 'And you're right, I like to look after them.' He bent and kissed her there, his tongue circling in ever-teasing strokes, before sliding inside.

Mya had given up on her analysis the moment he touched her. Her eyes closed as sensation rippled out from deep within her. He turned her on so quickly.

When she was wrung out and panting he rose, wearing the smile of a victor. She wound her arms around his waist and pulled him close.

'Mmm,' he groaned appreciatively as she wriggled beneath him. 'I've discovered a liking for clinging flowers.'

'What about carnivorous ones?' She arched swiftly and ate him whole.

But later as she tumbled towards sleep in his arms she reminded herself exactly how long this fling was going to last. Brad might have said no limitations, but as far as she was concerned it was for one week and one week only. She only had two lecture-free weeks over the Christmas break. The first was his, the second was for her assignments and exam study. There'd be no room for him in her life from then on. Abstinence had failed; an overdose had to work. One week of indulgence.

CHAPTER TEN

SHE came to him every night. And every night it was the same but different—variations on a theme. So many, many wonderful variations. He delighted in his deepening knowledge of her—he sought to learn what she liked, what made her shiver, the slow discovery of all her secrets. But finding enough time to see her was hard. Frantic sex followed by sleep followed by more frantic sex before she left for work. He sometimes had lunch with her—a snatched ten minutes before he was due in court or before she had a lecture. Ten minutes wasn't enough. He went back to the bar in the early evenings but then left to get more work done—and to let her work.

There wasn't enough time. Mya grasped the few moments they had but it felt like the glitter from the party—impossible to catch and hold. Just an ephemeral, beautiful shimmer. So she was determined to make the most of it. Brad seemed more intent than ever on 'just having fun' too—as if he was also aware of how brief this would be.

She stretched in his big bed, slowly and so reluctantly coming awake after what felt like only five minutes' sleep. She could hear him talking—dozily she listened to one half of an incisive discussion on some point of

law. She smiled as she snoozed. He sounded so authori-
tative—which he was on this, of course—quoting from
case after case, and given that she could hear he was
pacing down the far end of the hall, she knew he was
recalling those cases from his own memory, not that of
a computer. Geek. Question was why he was talking so
early in the morning.

She sat up and looked at her watch. It wasn't just early
in the morning—it was still the middle of the night.
She'd really had only a little more than five minutes'
sleep.

She slipped out of bed and wrapped a towel round
herself and tiptoed down the hall. She could see the light
in his office was on, and she paused in the doorway. He
stood at his desk, his hair a crumpled mess, unshaven,
circles under his eyes, still on that difficult call.

She took a step back and went back to the bedroom,
not wanting to eavesdrop. But in the silent house, his
voice carried—his concern was obvious. She waited
a very long time for him to return to bed. But even
though he'd stopped talking quite some time ago now,
he still didn't come down the hall. So she got up again—
concerned.

From in his office doorway, she saw him sitting at
his desk, his face a portrait of worry. She'd noticed before how tired he sometimes looked when he thought
no one was watching. The animated, charming façade
slipped on when people talked to him. She didn't want
him to feel as if he had to put that mask on for her. She
understood now that he covered up with the charm factor. Why did he feel the need to maintain the image?
When he claimed to hate that manufactured perfection
in his parents' home? In a way he was as guilty of it as
they were.

But then he closed his eyes and put his head in his hands.

'Brad?' She swiftly walked into the room, round the side of his desk and put her arms around him. It was an instinctive, caring gesture. Nothing sexual, just the comfort of a hug. 'What's wrong?'

For a long time he said nothing. But then there was a sigh and a mumble. 'Christmas is bad for most of my kids.'

My kids. The word meant much. She softened inside. He cared deeply, but he didn't like to display it for everyone. 'Something's happened?'

'Gage has run away.'

Mya bit her lip. Two days out from Christmas? Things must be bad. 'Who's Gage?'

'A client. His parents split a while back. He's been shuttling between them for a few years, but it's never been easy. His father had a new partner on the scene but they've split up recently.' He sighed. 'What's worse, do you think? Being fought over, or not being noticed or wanted at all?' He glanced at her. 'Or being expected to carry the expectations and dreams and ambitions of generations?'

She shook her head. 'It depends.'

'It does,' he said tiredly. 'I should have spotted there was something badly wrong,' he added quietly. 'I should have seen it. I knew he'd been truanting. I knew he hadn't been talking to the psych. But I—'

'You're not his parent.'

'I'm his advocate. I should know what it is he wants.'

'And do you?'

He stared sightlessly at the desk. 'I'm not sure. He's on the run but if I were to guess I'd say he'll head to his dad's ex. She's been the one there. But she lives in an-

other town now. She wasn't married to the guy. She's not
a guardian. In theory she has no legal claim to Gage.'

'But if he wants to stay with her, if she wants him—
can you help them?'

'Maybe. That's if he is heading there, if he is okay.'
He looked worried. 'Not all stepmothers are wicked.'

And not all playboys were heartless.

'It's really sad,' she said.

He nodded. 'And if he doesn't turn up soon, he's only
going to make it harder for himself to get what he wants.'

'I'm sorry, Brad.'

He rubbed his forehead, as if he could rub away the
stress. 'You should go get some sleep.'

'Not without you.' There was one thing she could
give him—the one thing he'd wanted from her. It wasn't
much, but it was all she had, and she wanted to give him
comfort now. She didn't know how she was going to do
it, but after Christmas she was walking away from him.
She'd been such a fool to think she could handle this.
'You do an incredible job,' she whispered. He was an
incredible person.

'Not good enough,' he muttered. 'Not this time. I
should have spotted it, Mya. Hell, I hope he's okay.'

'He will be.' She hugged him tighter. 'Don't feel bad,'
she urged. 'You help so many people. You'll help him
too.'

Worry burdened Brad—burned inside him. Because
he feared Mya was wrong—on several levels. 'I do this
job to make myself feel good. To pretend to myself that
I have helped out in some way,' he confessed. 'But do I
really?' He shrugged. 'Who knows?'

'Of course you do,' she said vehemently. 'You're
hugely talented and you give that talent to the most vulnerable. You're generous.'

'Mya,' he muttered, trying to claw back some cool. To joke his way out of this intensity the way he always did. 'I thought I only did counsel for child to score chicks?'

'I don't think you're as selfish as you like to make out that you are.'

Oh, but she was wrong. He knew he was selfish. He'd been told it many times by women. And they were right. 'I'm not very good company tonight.' He felt uncomfortable—felt vulnerable with her this moment. He wanted to pull it back in. His chest ached. Maybe he was coming down with summer flu. 'I don't feel that great,' he muttered, too tired to hold that last fact back.

'I know.'

He turned and looked at her—beautiful, bright, *sweet* Mya, whom he wanted so much from and yet who couldn't give it.

Wasn't it ironic that the game-changing woman for him didn't want the game changed? He'd positioned himself as her bed-buddy—painted himself into a corner as her 'good-time guy'. And was that so bad? A few minutes of fun here and there in an otherwise hardworking life? He was the king of quick'n'fun, wasn't he? With the same woman for once, yet what difference did that really make?

It made all the difference. Tonight it hurt.

Because he cared for her a lot more than he'd like, and the reality was he didn't stand a chance. There was no room in her life for him. Her parents came first and that was fair enough. He'd played the playboy role too well for too long for her to see him any other way. He supposed it served him right. But this second he was so wrung out, he was at the point where he'd take all he could get. And so he tried to pull it back on again—

his playful tease. 'Is there something you wanted?' he drawled.

But she didn't respond with the same kind of light amusement. 'Yes, there is.'

She didn't tease him with her wishes or do a pretend strip to reveal her polka-dotted panties and mismatched cotton bra. Instead she looked serious. 'Tell me what you want me to do.'

He coughed; it felt as if something were crushing his chest. A crazy, over-the-top reaction. This was hardly the first time a woman had asked him to reveal a sexual fantasy. But he didn't want a fantasy tonight. He just wanted Mya. 'I thought I made it clear you didn't have to do anything other than just be for me.'

'No. You've done what I wanted you to do so many times. Now it's your turn. I'm yours. What would you like me to do?'

He didn't answer. Frankly, he couldn't think with the way she was looking at him with all the promises of the world in her eyes and the sweetness in that unique smile.

'No ropes?' Finally, she teased. And her laughter tied his tongue—and his heart—the way no real binds ever could.

All he wanted was for her to welcome him the way she always did. All he needed was to see how much she enjoyed being with him; her response told him she was as enthralled as much as he in the passion between them. He ached for that total embrace, the softness in her body. Yeah, her embrace alone was enough. Her absolute acceptance. He took her hand and pulled her closer.

'Cover me,' he whispered.

Deliverance finally came as she draped her warm limbs over his.

CHAPTER ELEVEN

SHE never got back from the bar until the early hours of the morning. Brad loathed the thought of her walking home alone, but she refused to let him pick her up after work, arguing it was too late for him. She wouldn't pay for taxi fares—certainly wouldn't let *him* pay for them. According to her, her scream-in-a-can and night-school self-defence moves were enough protection. Not for Brad they weren't. She didn't know it but he'd paid Kirk, the bouncer, to walk her home these past couple of weeks. He'd even concocted the lie for Kirk to tell her—that he'd moved into the city and walking her wasn't far out of his way. Mya hadn't argued much, which made Brad suspect she wasn't completely convinced about her self-defence skills either. It made his blood sizzle that he could only help her if he did it secretly.

His blood sizzled more because of the intensity with which he *wanted* to help her. It was crazy. And even crazier was that here he was, awake way beyond midnight, waiting to hear the sound of the key in the lock. Since when had he *ever* given a woman a key to his home?

He'd seen how tired she was today. She'd had two coffees for breakfast this morning. He knew she'd get something to eat at the café—and more coffee. Then she'd gone straight into her shift at the bar. She'd get more sustenance there too. But what the woman needed was some sleep. She needed to take better care of herself. He needed to take better care of her. He hated how hard she worked. And he hated how it had been his fault she'd had so little sleep last night—and not from energetic bedroom games but talking. Off-loading all his troubles about Gage. He didn't feel comfortable about that either. It was time to ease back a bit, get them back into the playful groove. Lighten it up the way he liked it. But his mood was bleak—worried about Gage, worried about Mya, and, frankly, worried about himself and his ability to handle it all.

Eventually he heard her arrive, her heels clipping along the hallway. He rolled onto his stomach and closed his eyes, feigning deep sleep—too late to switch the light off.

'Brad?'

A stage whisper that he ignored. He counted his breathing, trying to keep it deep and regular.

She touched his shoulder, and he braced to stop the flinch as her fingertips stroked. She had a soft touch, but not shy. He made the counting in his head louder so he wouldn't smile. The thing she needed most right now was sleep, not an hour getting physical with him.

'Brad?'

He was *asleep*; hadn't she got that already?

She sighed. The edge of disappointment nearly broke his resolve. He'd make it up to her tomorrow. He'd disable her alarm and let her sleep late. Then he'd wake her slow—morning sex was the way to start the day, and they'd never yet managed it in any kind of leisurely fashion. And Christmas morning meant the café would be closed.

She walked a couple of paces away. He carefully opened his eyes and saw her back was to him. He could see the weariness in her shoulders, in the way she rubbed her forehead as if there was a residual ache there before she began to undress. He wished she wouldn't work as hard as she did. He wished she'd damn well let him help her out. She could drop one of her jobs; he'd see to it that she didn't starve.

He was so busy thinking he didn't notice that she'd turned around. Or that he was supposed to be out like a light.

'You're awake.'

He snapped his eyes shut but he knew it was too late.

'Brad!'

Busted. 'I was asleep.'

'You were pretending to be asleep!' She sounded out-raged. 'Why were you pretending to be asleep?' She sup-plied the answer before he could even open his mouth. 'You didn't want to have to perform tonight? You're lying there feigning sleep like some unfulfilled spouse trying to avoid duty sex?'

'Mya—'

'Are you bored already?'

It was the hurt behind the indignance that got him moving. He shot out of bed. 'Does it look like I'm bored?'

His erection was so hard it hurt, his skin pulled tighter than ever before. All he wanted to do was bury himself deep in her heat and find the release. He wanted those sensations that only she could give, to steal away all the thoughts that tormented him, to be as close as they'd been last night with nothing between them.

'If you didn't want me to come tonight, all you had to do is tell me.' She ignored his evidential display.

'I want you to come.' And yes, he meant that in the teenage double-entendre way.

'Then what are you doing pretending you're asleep?' Arms folded, foot tapping, she waited.

He sighed. He was a condemned man. His answer would annoy her but she wouldn't let him get away with not explaining himself to her. 'I thought you needed some sleep.'

Her jaw dropped.

'Look at you,' he said. 'You're exhausted.'

'The shadows beneath my eyes are a turn-off, is that it?' she queried—not hiding the hint of hurt. 'You're not doing a lot for my ego here.'

'Mya,' he said coaxingly and reached for her.

She pulled back out of reach. Totally put out. 'I work two jobs and study on top of that, so exhaustion is normal. I'm sorry if I can't live up to the high-gloss appearance of your usual lovers. Maybe you need to stick to ladies of leisure.'

'Mya.' He tried to laugh it off, gesturing at his erection. 'It's perfectly clear your appearance is still lethal for me.'

She wasn't buying it. 'You can't tell me you didn't pull some all-nighters when you were studying. It's normal student behaviour.'

'Not every assignment, I didn't.'

'Well, bully for you for being more organised than me.'

'No one can be more organised than you. Your problem is that not only are you studying, you're working two jobs. That's not a normal workload.'

'In my world it happens all the time. You do what you have to do.'

'Yeah, but *you* don't have to do that much.'

'I do if I need to eat.'

'Why not let me help you?'

She whirled away from him. 'You don't need to help me. All I want from you is—'

'Yeah, okay. I got it.' He didn't want to hear what *little* she wanted from him. He'd made the bed. But now the bed wasn't enough for him.

What was wrong with him? He'd never turned down sex. Ever. If a pretty woman was offering, he was on it. Easy come, easy go and a good time had by both.

She'd wanted to ravish him, and he'd lain there like a log. And ironically harder than a piece of petrified wood. He'd definitely come down with some kind of mind-altering fever. And now she was halfway down the hallway again.

'You're not leaving,' he stated, striding after her.

'I'm not staying where I'm not wanted.'

'You're wanted. You *know* you're wanted. All you have to do is look at me to know you're wanted.'

'That's just a normal state of being for you.'

White-hot fury ripped through him because this was *not* normal for him.

She turned in time to read his expression and suddenly shook her head. 'Don't make this complicated.' She kept backing up the hallway. 'I think I'll spend tonight at my place. Catch up on my beauty sleep.' A pointed look. 'And I need to get to my parents' place early in the morning. We can get together next week.'

He caught up to her in a couple of quick strides. He

pulled her against him and kissed her until she was panting. And so was he.

'You couldn't look more beautiful than you do right now,' he said.

When her attention was riveted on him. When desire filled her eyes and blood pounded in her lips and she was seconds off breathing his name.

But that hurt look in her eyes grew—dimming that light. 'You just don't like me walking out on you right now. But you started it.'

'What I don't like is how hard you're working. Why not work smarter instead of harder?'

'What is that piece of management-mag speak supposed to mean?'

'Get just one job. A better job. Get an internship at a firm.'

She shook her head.

'You could clerk for me over the summer.' It was the worst thing to suggest; he knew it before he'd even opened his mouth but he couldn't stop the words.

'I'm not a charity case. I'm tired of charity. I want to do it myself. I want to deserve it myself.'

'You do deserve it,' he argued, his volume lifting along with his frustration. 'You're super smart. You've got amazing grades. Any firm would want you.'

'You only do because of this...connection,' she said. 'It's the sexual equivalent of the old boys' network. Only because you know me. I'd rather send my CV out and get a job on my own merit.'

'Okay, fine. Will you send your CV to my firm?'

'Of course not.'

'So you're doing the opposite. Because we do know each other, you won't work with me?'

'We couldn't. I couldn't.'

'Why not? We'd make a great team.'

She just stared at him.

'Everybody makes connections, Mya,' he said, his body clenched with frustration. Wanting to shake sense into her some way or another and knowing already that he was doomed to failure. She was so *damn* obstinate. 'That's why they have networking groups. Young lawyers, young farmers, young fashion designers. People have mentors. It's normal.'

'You set up on your own,' she argued. 'You turned your back on any help your father could offer.'

He drew a hard breath. 'You know I had my reasons for that. And I still had help. I might have turned my back on my father's help, but I still had his name.' He sighed. 'And to be honest I know that helped. It helped that I had money.'

'It helped more that you'd won all the prizes in your year at university. Your own merit, Brad. I want to do the same.'

'I still had help,' he ground out through his teeth, hating to have to admit it, but knowing it was the truth.

'Well, I'll get my lecturer to write a reference or something.'

'So it's just me you won't accept help from?'

'I'm not using our personal relationship for professional gain.'

'So we have a relationship.' He pounced.

'No,' she denied instantly, swallowing hard. 'This is a fling. Stress relief.' Mya stared at him in all his naked glory. What was the man thinking? Why was he changing the rules—why was he offering for her to work with him? As if that were possible? What did he think would happen when he decided he'd had enough of sleeping with her? No way could she take this from him.

'Look, I made the mistake of going for one job based on a relationship already. I'm not doing it again. James had suggested I apply for an internship at a particular firm last summer.' She'd been thrilled when they'd both been accepted. 'But then he found out some of my grades and I took him home to see my parents...and it was like he turned into a different person overnight.' It wasn't until later that she learned how average James's grades really were. 'But his grades didn't matter because he was getting a job at the most prestigious accountancy firm in town anyway because his dad was a partner there. Meanwhile I spent my first pay packet in advance buying clothes that might possibly be acceptable to work there, but after he broke up with me, and just before those exams, the company withdrew the offer, saying they had no need for so many interns. So no, I'm not trusting any job offer based on any kind of connection other than merit. I'm not having any kind of relationship interfere with my future.'

'So you have to earn everything yourself? You can't accept a gift? I only have money thanks to *chance* at birth. You can't take anything from me?' he asked, completely frustrated.

'That's right.' She wouldn't take anything from him. Because what he was offering wouldn't ever be enough. 'I need to earn it myself.'

'You have to be so independent, don't you? You have to be the best,' he said bitterly. 'So insanely competitive you're on the brink of a breakdown from the sleepless nights and caffeine overdoses. Well, why don't you go ahead and study yourself to death? Then work yourself to death and become a corporate lawyer.'

'Is that such a crime?'

'It is when you have huge talent in another area.'

She rolled her eyes. 'Don't go there.'

'You should make time for your wearable art. It's important to you. You should be happy as well as successful.'

That wasn't what was going to make her happy.

'It's something you're so good at,' he continued. 'You should take the opportunity. You should put your work out there.'

'I can't.'

'You'd rather not compete at all rather than come second?' He shook his head. 'Is being the best *so* important to you?'

'Success requires sacrifice,' she said firmly. 'What would you have me do, Brad? Give up all I've worked so hard for, to try and scrape a living selling some recycled tat? That's not realistic. It's not going to happen. Yes, I love doing that but I also love the law.'

'So strike a *balance*.'

'I can't yet.'

'You won't ever,' he said, going quiet. 'There'll always be something else you feel you have to achieve. Your parents wouldn't want you to live like this. Your parents want you to be happy.'

'Don't talk to me about what my parents want. I know what they *need*.' And she was the only one who could help them.

'You don't. You can't face up to what *you* need, let alone anyone else,' he argued. 'You lie to your parents.

What's worse is you lie to yourself. You're so scared of failing you can't take any kind of real risk.'

'And you can?' So hurt, she poured it all back on him. '*You're* the one who constantly has to be the epitome of charm. You're as bad as your parents. You project this perfect façade—all funny and capable and unable to admit to anything being wrong or *needing* anything. *You're* the one who's scared. You're the one who can't take any kind of support.' She paused and saw he'd gone pale.

He drew in a deep breath but she didn't give him the chance to try to argue—because there was no argument. 'We want different things, Brad,' she said sadly.

He didn't answer. And she turned and left.

CHAPTER TWELVE

As DAWN broke on Christmas Day, Gage Simmons pushed his blistered feet and aching back onward. He knocked on the door. She opened it in less than a minute—the woman he wish, wish, *wished* were his mother. The one he'd walked miles and miles to get to. The one he wanted to stay with. The one who'd shown him more love and compassion and simple fun than any of his blood relatives.

'Will it be okay?' His voice wobbled as she pulled him into a super-tight hug.

'I don't know,' she murmured into his hair. 'But we're going to try.' For a moment they watched the sunrise together. 'We have to call them, you know. It's not fair on your parents not knowing where you are.'

Gage closed his eyes and thought none of it was fair. But he nodded.

'Look at the day, Gage.' She kept her arm around him. 'It's going to be a beauty.'

He didn't want the sun to move. It had taken so long to find her and he didn't want to leave. Not yet. He didn't want another second to pass.

'We'll work it out, Gage. I promise.'

* * *

There was a single-sentence mention in the morning news bulletin—that the boy who'd gone missing had been located and was well. Mya desperately wanted to call Brad and ask if everything truly was okay. But it wasn't okay enough between them for her to be able to do that. And there was something else she had to do— urgently.

Utterly sleep-deprived, Mya walked up the overgrown path towards her parents' house. She'd fantasised for so long about turning up there with a property deed in hand tied by a ribbon. Her gift to them—a Christmas gift. Wouldn't that be wonderful? To be able to move them somewhere so much better. And she would do it; one day she would. It just wouldn't be as soon as she'd hoped it might. And she was so sorry she hadn't been able to be everything they'd wanted her to be.

Brad was right, she had lied—to her parents and to herself about what she really wanted. Because she was so scared of letting them down and of being let down herself.

She sat on the sofa and told them—about losing the scholarship, about working two jobs on top of summer school, about what she wanted to do for them more than anything.

Her parents were appalled, but not for the reason she'd feared.

'We wouldn't expect you to do that for us!' her mother cried. 'We're okay here.'

'You're not.' Mya wiped her own tears away. 'I wanted to do this for you so much. I wanted you to be so proud of me and I've let you down.'

'You've never let us down,' her father argued gruffly.

'We let you down. I gave up. I got injured and gave up and put all our hopes on you. That wasn't fair.'

'No wonder you're so thin and tired,' her mother exclaimed, rubbing Mya's shoulder. 'All we want for you is to be happy.' She put her arms around her. 'What would make you happy?'

So many things—her parents' comfort now certainly helped. There was that other thing too—but she didn't think he was hers to have.

'Can we get rid of all those photos of me winning prizes?' Mya half laughed and pushed her fringe from her eyes, determined to focus on the future and fixing things with her family.

'They bother you?'

Mya nodded. They took down most of them together, leaving a few, finding a few others with the three of them together. The cousins turned up, and the Christmas eat-a-thon began. As the day faded, Mya picked up the discarded lid from a soda bottle and started playing with it, twisting it—tempted for the first time in ages to create something silly-but-stylish just for the sake of it.

Brad was almost two hours late getting to his parents' place for the obligatory big Christmas lunch. The calls between Gage and his stepmother and his parents and their lawyers had gone on and on until they'd wrangled a solution for today at least. Gage would stay with his 'stepmother' until this afternoon, when he'd have time with each parent.

Poor kid. But at least now Brad knew what his client wanted, where he wanted to be and who he wanted to be with. He'd demonstrated it in an extreme way, but Brad was determined they'd work it out. He'd not stop working on it until they did.

He walked into the ridiculously decorated home and spied Lauren looking sulky at the overloaded table. He

wasn't in the least hungry and stared at the twenty perfect platters of food for the four of them. Hell, it was the
last thing he felt like—some fake happy-family thing.
Surely there was a better use for them today?

'Why don't we take all this food down to the local
homeless shelter?' he asked his mother.

She looked appalled.

'We can't eat it all.' Brad shrugged. 'Honestly, Mother,
what's the point? Let's do something decent with it.'

He looked at his mother, who looked at his father,
who said nothing.

'Great idea,' said Lauren, standing up.

'Okay,' said his mother slowly.

'I'm not that hungry anyway,' his father commented.

'Good,' Brad said. 'Why don't you two go down together to deliver it?' He stared at his parents, who both
stared, rather aghast, back at him.

'That's more your mother's scene,' his father eventually said.

'It's Christmas Day,' Brad answered firmly. 'You
should be together.' He moved forward. It'd be a relief
to escape the picture-perfect scene with the empty un-
dercurrents. 'We'll *all* go.'

Open-mouthed, Lauren watched him gather up a couple of platters.

'Come on,' Brad said insistently. 'Let's do it.'

He was surprised that they actually did. They loaded
all the food into his father's car, and Brad and Lauren
followed in Brad's car.

For two hours they stood and served food to the people who'd come to the shelter. Their platters had gone
into the mix, and his parents were now fully engaged
in dishwashing duty.

'This was so much better than a strained dinner with them,' Lauren muttered under her breath.

'I know,' Brad agreed. 'Genius. But are you hungry now?'

'Yeah, but not for any kind of roast.' She looked slightly guilty. 'How bad is that?'

'Why don't we go get Chinese?' he suggested with a half-laugh. 'The restaurant round the corner from me does really good yum char.'

'Shouldn't we have dinner with Mum and Dad?'

'Nah, let's leave them to it. We've done enough family bonding for the day.'

'I actually think they're happy the way they are,' Lauren said as she pulled a chicken dish towards her, half an hour later.

'You think?' Brad asked.

'Yes.' Lauren chewed thoughtfully. 'Surely if they weren't, they'd have done something about it by now?'

'I think they're just used to it.' He sat back and toyed with the food on his plate. 'They're apathetic and simply don't care enough to do anything to change things.'

'It's a waste,' Lauren said.

'It is,' Brad agreed. 'Maybe they'll learn something at the shelter.' He grinned. 'It might be a Christmas miracle.'

Lauren suddenly looked serious. 'Have you seen Mya recently?'

Brad's moment of lightness fled. He shook his head and stuffed rice into his mouth to keep from having to answer.

'She's not really a sister to you, is she?' Lauren said slyly.

The observation caught him by surprise—he half laughed, half choked and shook his head again.

'Is it going to work out?'

He shook his head again—slower that time.

'Have you stuffed things up so badly I'm going to lose my best friend?'

He shook his head more vehemently. 'Be there for her.'

Lauren studied him closely. 'Why can't you be?'

'She doesn't want me to.'

'Really?' Lauren frowned. 'Mya had a thing for you for years. Even when you never saw her.'

Yeah, but the trouble was Mya had got to know him properly now. And though he'd offered her all he could, she'd turned him down. It hurt.

'Don't tell me you're too apathetic to do anything about it, Brad,' Lauren said softly. 'Don't make the same mistake as Mum and Dad.'

Lauren's words haunted him over the next week. The memory of Mya positively tortured him. Night after night he replayed their last conversation in his head and he dreamed of the too few nights they'd been together.

She'd been furious with him for not opening up. She claimed he maintained as much of a false façade as his parents did. He'd not realised he did that. But she was right. He had opened up to her, though—a couple of times he had, and she'd been there for him in a way that had made his heart melt. So why was it that when he'd wanted to support her, she'd pushed him away? Until now he'd been too hurt to try to figure it out, but now he had to *know*.

Lauren was right too: he couldn't be apathetic. He needed courage—Gage's kind of courage. To run to-wards what you needed most—the one person you needed most. The one whose love and laughter meant everything.

He went to the bar and pushed forward to the front of the bar section she was serving. Her eyes widened when she saw him and she asked his order ahead of the people he was standing beside. He refused to get a kick out of that—it was probably because she wanted to serve him so he'd leave asap.

He inhaled the sight of her like a man gulping fresh air after a long, deep dive in the abyss. And as she mixed his deliberately complicated cocktail, he tried for conversation. 'I like your hairclip.' So lame. But true.

She put her hand to her head where her homemade clip resided and smiled self-consciously. 'You do?'

'Absolutely.'

She nodded, looking down to stir some awful collection of liqueurs before speaking quickly. 'I don't have the time right now for entire outfits,' she said. 'But hair accessories I can do. Pretty clips, small statements. Just a little fun and it keeps my fringe out of my eyes.'

'That's great.'

'It's enough,' she said. 'But you were right. I needed it.'

'Good for you.' He wished she needed him too.

For a moment their eyes met, and Brad was too tired to hide anything any more. He was too tired to try to make chit-chat and break the bulletproof wall of ice between them. He just wanted to hold her close—to have her in his arms and by his side and have it all. For ever.

But she moved to serve another person, and it was like having scabs from third-degree body burns ripped off. Coming here was the dumbest thing he'd done. For a guy who was supposed to be smart, he'd picked the world's worst time to try to talk to her. New Year's Eve was the busiest night of the year. Jonny was back—there were five bartenders there and all of them run off their feet. And she couldn't even look him in the eye.

He didn't even touch the cocktail she'd made for him. He just turned round and walked away.

Mya glanced up from making the next customer's cocktail—desperate to make sure he was still there. But he wasn't. She stretched up on tiptoe and just got a glimpse of his back heading towards the exit.

Oh, no. No, no and no. He wasn't turning up for the first time in a week looking all rough-edged and danger-ous and for one heart-stopping moment *vulnerable*—and then leaving again. She had things to say to him. Things she'd been rehearsing in her head for days and days and no matter the outcome she was still determined to say.

She pushed her way out from behind the bar and barged through the throngs. 'Brad!' She didn't care who heard her.

But if he did hear her, he didn't stop. She ran out onto the footpath and charged after him. 'Brad!'

This time he stopped.

She looked at him, oblivious to the revellers on the street and the heat in the summer night. And now all those words that she'd been mentally practising just flew out of her head—when he looked at her like *that*?

'Oh, hell, don't cry,' he groaned.

'I'm not *crying*!' she denied. And then sniffed. So what was the point in denial? 'Okay, I'm…crying.'

'Mya.' He sounded strangled. 'Please go back.'

'Mya! Drew is having a fit.' Kirk came puffing up beside them. 'We need you back at the bar.'

'I don't give a damn about the bar,' Mya snapped.

Kirk scuttled away like a dirt bug escaping daylight.

'Mya, you should go back. You don't want to lose your job.'

'I don't, but—'

'And you need to focus on your upcoming exam.'

'I don't give a damn about that exam either!' she shouted.

Brad stared at her, waiting.

'Okay, I do, but...' She broke off to draw a ragged breath. 'I don't care about the bar. But I do. I don't care about the exam. But I do. I don't care about anything that much but *you*,' she admitted softly. 'And I don't want you to walk away from me.' Another fat tear spilt down her cheek.

He sighed and took a step towards her. 'Mya, I've always believed that no one can ever truly put another person first. That ultimately we're all selfish and do what's best for ourselves. But I was wrong about that.' He stopped and breathed out. 'Because I will do whatever *you* need me to do in order for you to be happy. If that means walking out of your life, then that's what I'll do. It's the last thing I want to do. But I want what's best for you.'

She shook her head angrily. 'You might be brilliant but you're not a mind-reader. What makes you think walking out of my life would be best for me?'

'It's what you asked me to do,' he pointed out.

'Well, I was an idiot.'

He stared at her. 'What do you want me to do?'

'I don't know that you can offer me what I really want from you.'

'I know you want to hold onto your independence. I respect that. If you want the big corporate law job, then fantastic. I'll suck up my stupid fears and be right there behind you. If you decide you'd rather make your creations and try selling them, I can afford to support you. You can ask me for anything,' he said.

She shook her head. She didn't want any *thing*. 'I can't

be dependent on you. I just can't.' She couldn't give herself so completely to a guy who didn't feel the same for her as she did for him.

'You want me to give it all away?' he suddenly exploded. 'Okay, I'll give all my money away. I'll give a guy the shirt on my back and stand here naked and with nothing. I just want to support you,' he roared at her. 'And you won't take it from me!'

'It's not your money I want!' she shouted back. 'It's everything else. You have *everything* to give me. Love and *emotional* support, rather than financial. Strength. Humour. Play. Everything that's so wonderful about you. I love you and all I want is for you to love me back.'

He stared at her. Stunned. 'Why didn't you tell me?' He gestured wide. 'You never showed me. You never wanted anyone to know about us. You were embarrassed to want me.'

'I was never embarrassed about wanting you. What was I supposed to do? You're the ultimate playboy. Never with any woman more than a week. I had to protect myself somehow. I had to think of it as just a fantasy. If no one else knew then it wasn't really real.'

He gazed at her, now motionless. 'What do you think I feel for you?'

'Lust.'

'Absolutely. Lust is right up there. Right now so is annoyance.' He walked towards her. 'Also admiration. Frustration. But above all, love.'

She bent her head.

He put his fingers under her chin and lifted her face back up to his. 'Mya, why do you think I want to give you everything I have?' He gazed into her eyes. 'I love you more than I've ever loved anyone. Even myself,' he joked just that little bit.

'Brad,' she choked out.

'Has it not occurred to you that I'm the best person to help you with your studies?'

She laughed, but it was in despair. 'I failed so badly at concentrating that night you found those cases for me. I had the wickedest thoughts going on that night. I can't concentrate with you around.'

'We weren't sleeping together then. We were both frustrated. Wouldn't it be different knowing you can have your way with me when your study goal is met? Won't it be different now you know I love you and that you love me? And that we can be together as much as we want?'

Yeah, she still couldn't quite believe that.

He muttered something unintelligible and then just swept her close, his lips crashing onto hers as if there were no other way to convince her. And she *ached* to be convinced, desperate to feel the security that should only be a breath away. She burrowed closer, opening for him, wanting to give him everything and get it all in return.

'Do I really have to give away my money?' he asked gently. 'If I was a starving student, you'd share every-thing with me, right?'

'Of course. But you're not a starving student. It feels so unbalanced.' She sighed.

'Only in that one aspect and that's only temporary. In another couple of years you'll be qualified and raking it in, and I'll take early retirement and you can keep me in the manner to which I am accustomed.'

She couldn't help it, laughter bubbled out of her. 'And in what manner is that?'

'Restaurant meals every night,' he said promptly.

'I can do salads from the café down the street.'

'Sex every night of the week.' He waggled his brows.

'And every morning.'

'That too.' He kissed her again. 'You were right, by the way. I do my job because it makes me feel better about myself as a person. I tell myself I'm okay because I help kids. I make a difference, right? So I can't be all bad.' He sighed. 'But I'm not all that great. I chose not to get too close to anyone and never let anyone see behind the façade. That was because, like you, I don't like failure. Growing up in that house with my parents, I saw the falseness of their relationship. Swore I'd never have such a marriage. And that I'd never fail kids like that. That I'd never have them.'

'You don't want to commit. I know that.' She'd never try to fence him in. She'd have him for as long as he was hers to have. No way she could walk away from him now.

He laughed. 'I don't have the choice, darling,' he teased. 'I'm not interested in anyone else. I don't want to be. I want this to work with you. You inspire me to be more.'

'I'm not some perfect creature.' She shook her head.

'No one is. But you kill yourself *trying* to be perfect and you don't have to. You don't have to get the top grade. You don't have to be the best bartender in town. You don't have to excel at everything. You can fail at everything and I'll love you anyway. Do you understand that? I'll love you no matter what.'

Her eyes filled as she felt the intensity of his words, the full emotion behind them. And finally she did understand that.

'You're wonderful and human, and you make mistakes like I do, but you pick yourself up and you fight on,' he said. 'You face your failures and you get it together.'

'I don't fight on,' she cried. 'I gave up on you, on us, before we'd hardly started. I was so scared. I didn't want to change my priorities only to find out what we had wasn't anything more than a bit of fun.'

'It's a whole lot of fun.' He smiled. 'And you don't have to change your priorities. We can have so much more fun together if you'll take a chance on me.'

He stood before her, his expression open, no protective façade in place, just pure honesty and an offer she could never, ever refuse.

Now she saw behind his mask to the genuine, loving man he was. While he could act all cocky, come up with the most outrageous statements as if he fully believed he was God's gift to the female of the species, beneath that bravado was a guy as insecure as any other normal person. Despite that silver spoon, that money, all that success…there was still someone who doubted that another person could love him for just being him. But that was the part of him she loved the most.

'I need nothing but you,' she answered simply.

And he needed someone who didn't give a damn about anything he had, or his image. A person who cared only about him. The *essence* of him. The good-humoured, gorgeous, arrogant guy.

Happily that someone was her.

She wrapped her arms around him and lifted her face for another kiss. Offering her heart. It was a long time before he drew back and sighed. She felt the elation in every inch of him, but also the tension.

'You need to go back and finish your shift,' he groaned. 'New Year's Eve is the biggest night of the year.'

'It is.' She nodded. 'Will you wait for me?'

'Always.'

* * *

'We'll go on a two-hour rotation,' he said firmly the next morning after they'd had breakfast. 'Two hours' solid study, two hours' solid sex.'

'That's finding balance?' she asked incredulously.

'I think so.' He nodded in all seriousness. 'Round the clock.'

She giggled. 'Yeah, that's really achieving balance.'

'No point in trying to fight our natures, now, is there? Might as well roll with it.' He winked. 'Right now I'm on case names and caffeine duty. And then massage services.'

'Massage services?'

'Inside and out.' He lifted his brows lasciviously.

Deep inside her, muscles shifted, ready.

He laughed, reading her thoughts. 'Later, babe. You've got facts to memorise.'

How was she supposed to concentrate when she knew what was coming? She was insanely excited already. 'I think you should feel me up first.'

'No. Work now, reward later.' He put himself on the far side of the desk and refused to look at her.

She sighed and sat up in her seat, pulling her pages of notes closer. 'Better be a good reward,' she grumbled beneath her breath.

'Mya, darling,' he drawled from his desk. 'You know it's going to be out of this world.'

And it was.

TWO YEARS LATER

You know you want this.

Mya smothered a giggle at the photo she'd just been sent on her phone. Brad, buck naked and bold with a party hat magically positioned in a very strategic place.

She quickly closed the message and acted as if she were paying complete attention to the orientation speech for new recruits at the multinational law firm she'd signed with. But her phone vibrated again.

Tonight. Our place. Come as soon as you can.

As soon as the spiels and slideshows were over— as interesting as they were—she escaped. She walked through the city, the warm summer air delightful on her back. Her first week had gone well, long hours, of course, and that competitive component. She relished it. She loved coming home too. Especially to Brad in playboy mode.

'Brad?' She closed the front door and called down the cool empty hallway.

'In the garden,' came his distant shout.

She walked through the house, her footsteps ringing loud. The rest of the house unnaturally silent—until she stepped out onto the back deck.

'SURPRISE!'

There were five hundred people in the backyard.

Mya put out a hand and it was immediately gripped. Lauren laughed as she squeezed her hand to bring her back from the light-headed faint feeling.

'Oh, wow!' Mya couldn't move. Certainly couldn't think of anything to say.

'Breathe, woman, you need some colour back.'

It was already back. Mya felt the blush burning over every bit of her body. OMG, there was a huge surprise party. Here. For her.

Dazed, she glanced around.

Her family were there—her mother beaming, her father standing by the barbecue helping Stella turn the steaks. They were in a new home only about ten minutes away. Brad had insisted he help them as soon as they'd

got together that New Year's Eve two years ago. It had
made such a difference to her parents.

Jonny and Drew were there from the bar. Some of
her cousins were there, also beaming. Many of Lauren's
men. Brad's buddies. Some of her law school mates, a
whole mishmash of people from her life. And they were
all smiling, all celebrating, and they'd managed to keep
this whole thing secret from her?

But there was only the one person she really wanted
to see this second. And that was the tall hunk coming towards her through the crowd with a glass of champagne.

'You did all this?' she asked as he stepped unneces-
sarily close to hand the drink to her.

'You know what a good party planner I am.' He bent
to whisper in her ear and steal a kiss at the same time.
'But don't be disappointed—we'll have our own private
party a little later.'

She giggled. As if she could ever be disappointed!
And she knew that they'd have their own time tonight.
Everyone else would leave, but Brad would always be
there for her.

She sipped her champagne and stepped forward with
a smile, Brad alongside her.

She'd dropped the café work and many of the shifts at
the bar, working only during the weekends so she saved
the weeknights for the two of them. The nights she did
work, Brad came down to the bar and kept her company.
His gang of mates had been more than happy for it to
become their regular. And she'd gone back full-time at
university to finish her degree—with a promise to pay
Brad back sometime for all the free rent. He didn't bother
arguing or answering that one, just rolled his eyes.

She'd had four job offers before her final exams. She

didn't win the gold medal for top law graduate of the year, but she did take out the prize for top family law student. She'd thrown that in with all the contract and company law courses so she could understand what Brad was going on about in the evenings. He'd been right, he was a brilliant coach—firm, but he had a super-fun reward system going.

Yeah, she had the best prize already. She didn't think she could be happier.

She loved the party. There was no catwalk this time, no 'wall of fame' either. It was all friends and family and laughter.

His parents were there too. Mya chatted with them. They all worked the façade to a degree but Brad had become a lot more open about talking with them—quite blunt in some of his views. Mya backed him up. They were his parents, and if he could make that effort, so could she.

'I'm so proud of you.' She leaned back against him several hours later as they stood at the door and watched the last guests leave.

His laugh rumbled in his chest. 'That's my line.'

'I mean it.' She turned to face him, pressing her breasts against his strength. 'You're the most generous man I know.'

He laughed even harder. 'You have rose-tinted glasses.'

Her smile blossomed too. 'You grow the roses for me.'

He brushed his lips against hers and took a step backwards into the hall to close the door.

'I have a graduation present for you.' His breathing quickened.

'I haven't graduated yet.'

'Mere technicality.' He gifted her a teasingly light

kiss. 'I was going to give it to you when they were all here because I figured you couldn't refuse it in front of everyone. But then I thought that wasn't fair.' He put his hand in his jeans pocket and pulled out a box.

Her heart stopped. 'Brad—'

'Two years we've been together,' he interrupted mock crossly. 'Don't you think it's time you made an honest man of me?' He opened the box.

She went hot and cold and hot again in a nanosecond.

His hands gripped her shoulders as if he knew she'd gone light-headed. 'You can't take advantage of me so long. Taking what you want, when you want it. Demanding all those pictures of me and treating me like some kind of sex object.'

'And you're not?'

He shook his head, his eyes dancing. 'No, I need solid commitment from you. I want a public declaration. I want this rock flashing on your finger to show those pups at that law firm that you're taken. And I want a family.'

'Oh, you do?' Her sass answer was totally undermined by her breathless gasp.

'Yes.'

She took a moment to inhale a few times. 'Got anything else to add to this list of demands?'

'Speed,' he snapped. 'I want the big wedding as soon as possible. And one hell of a honeymoon. In fact—' he drew breath '—I've already started planning it.'

'The family?' Her voice rose. She was still getting to grips with that idea. She'd thought he never wanted kids.

'No, that part can wait 'til after you're crowned biggest fee earner at the firm and you've taken me on a round-the-world trip.' His reply was tinged with laughter.

She didn't care about being the biggest fee earner. She

cared about her parents and him and everybody staying well and happy. So happy. 'So it's the honeymoon you're planning?'

'No, the wedding. I've decided on the flowers already.' He winked.

She giggled. 'Well, we know party planning is your niche. You should jack in the law practice and just do parties.'

'Now, that wouldn't be fair on my clients.'

'No.' She sobered and placed her palm on the side of his face in the gentlest caress. 'They need you.' He'd worked so hard mediating with Gage's parents and the stepmother—finally hammering out a solution that had made that sombre-eyed boy so happy. She leaned closer. 'I need you too. More than I can ever tell you.'

'Same here.' He wrapped his arms around her and pulled her right into his heat. 'So that's a yes to my proposal, then?'

She rested her head on his chest. Her big, strong playboy loved her no matter what, supported her no matter what, and together they could build it all. 'Yes.'

'It's going to be one hell of a party, Mya,' he whispered.

Yes. One that would last the rest of their lives.

* * * * *

Mills & Boon® Hardback

December 2012

ROMANCE

A Ring to Secure His Heir	Lynne Graham
What His Money Can't Hide	Maggie Cox
Woman in a Sheikh's World	Sarah Morgan
At Dante's Service	Chantelle Shaw
At His Majesty's Request	Maisey Yates
Breaking the Greek's Rules	Anne McAllister
The Ruthless Caleb Wilde	Sandra Marton
The Price of Success	Maya Blake
The Man From her Wayward Past	Susan Stephens
Blame it on the Bikini	Natalie Anderson
The English Lord's Secret Son	Margaret Way
The Secret That Changed Everything	Lucy Gordon
Baby Under the Christmas Tree	Teresa Carpenter
The Cattleman's Special Delivery	Barbara Hannay
Secrets of the Rich & Famous	Charlotte Phillips
Her Man In Manhattan	Trish Wylie
His Bride in Paradise	Joanna Neil
Christmas Where She Belongs	Meredith Webber

MEDICAL

From Christmas to Eternity	Caroline Anderson
Her Little Spanish Secret	Laura Iding
Christmas with Dr Delicious	Sue MacKay
One Night That Changed Everything	Tina Beckett

Mills & Boon® Large Print

December 2012

ROMANCE

Contract with Consequences	Miranda Lee
The Sheikh's Last Gamble	Trish Morey
The Man She Shouldn't Crave	Lucy Ellis
The Girl He'd Overlooked	Cathy Williams
Mr Right, Next Door!	Barbara Wallace
The Cowboy Comes Home	Patricia Thayer
The Rancher's Housekeeper	Rebecca Winters
Her Outback Rescuer	Marion Lennox
A Tainted Beauty	Sharon Kendrick
One Night With The Enemy	Abby Green
The Dangerous Jacob Wilde	Sandra Marton

HISTORICAL

A Not So Respectable Gentleman?	Diane Gaston
Outrageous Confessions of Lady Deborah	Marguerite Kaye
His Unsuitable Viscountess	Michelle Styles
Lady with the Devil's Scar	Sophia James
Betrothed to the Barbarian	Carol Townend

MEDICAL

Sydney Harbour Hospital: Bella's Wishlist	Emily Forbes
Doctor's Mile-High Fling	Tina Beckett
Hers For One Night Only?	Carol Marinelli
Unlocking the Surgeon's Heart	Jessica Matthews
Marriage Miracle in Swallowbrook	Abigail Gordon
Celebrity in Braxton Falls	Judy Campbell

Mills & Boon® Hardback
January 2013

ROMANCE

Beholden to the Throne	Carol Marinelli
The Petrelli Heir	Kim Lawrence
Her Little White Lie	Maisey Yates
Her Shameful Secret	Susanna Carr
The Incorrigible Playboy	Emma Darcy
No Longer Forbidden?	Dani Collins
The Enigmatic Greek	Catherine George
The Night That Started It All	Anna Cleary
The Secret Wedding Dress	Ally Blake
Driving Her Crazy	Amy Andrews
The Heir's Proposal	Raye Morgan
The Soldier's Sweetheart	Soraya Lane
The Billionaire's Fair Lady	Barbara Wallace
A Bride for the Maverick Millionaire	Marion Lennox
Take One Arranged Marriage...	Shoma Narayanan
Wild About the Man	Joss Wood
Breaking the Playboy's Rules	Emily Forbes
Hot-Shot Doc Comes to Town	Susan Carlisle

MEDICAL

The Surgeon's Doorstep Baby	Marion Lennox
Dare She Dream of Forever?	Lucy Clark
Craving Her Soldier's Touch	Wendy S. Marcus
Secrets of a Shy Socialite	Wendy S. Marcus

Mills & Boon® Large Print

January 2013

ROMANCE

HISTORICAL

MEDICAL